MARIANNE REESE

SKYLAR MOON

REESE PUBLISHING
CALIFORNIA

Marianne Reese/Reese Publishing
mreeseauthor@gmail.com
https://mariannereeseauthor.wordpress.com

Publisher's Note: This is a work of fiction. Names, characters, places, and incidents are a product of the author's imagination. Locales and public names are sometimes used for atmospheric purposes. Any resemblance to actual people, living or dead, or to businesses, companies, events, institutions, or locales is completely coincidental.

Skylar Moon/Marianne Reese. – 2nd ed.
ISBN: 978-0-9994579-2-4

This one's for you, the reader.

Chapter One

The air chilled as they neared the open expanse of Ice Lake. Through the shadows of the trees they could see a layer of fog hovering above the water. The view was mystifying, yet naturally beautiful. At the shoreline was a rock formation with a flat granite slab atop two round boulders, perfect for sitting. The Bench, as they named it, was their destination. They never made it.

Nana Gazelle stopped dead in her tracks. Her violet eyes were wide with despair.

Aren, who had been rambling on about Emma, his new found interest at school, stopped mid-sentence when he realized there was something amiss. "Nana, what's wrong?"

"Her ears," Nana Gazelle said barely audible. Her finger trembled as she pointed towards Alexa, Aren's twin sister. Alexa had been walking several feet in front of them, listening with amusement as Aren stammered through asking Nana for permission to attend the school dance with Emma. Had Alexa not pulled her hair back and started rubbing at the tips of her slightly pointed ears Nana may not have noticed them.

Alexa asked, "What's wrong with my ears?" They were itching horribly.

Aren's eyes widened at the sight. "They're ... they're ... glowing!" stammered Aren. "They're turning red!"

The short gray hairs on the back of Nana's neck prickled. "Quiet!" she said. Her body tensed as a worried look covered her aging face. Nana Gazelle looked about, up in the trees and beyond the bushes. She saw nothing, but she could feel them. They were very near.

Suddenly, an eerie hush enveloped the woods. The air became very still as the breeze that had been flowing through the trees ceased, the birds stopped chirping, and all the natural noises of the forest seemed to vanish.

"Run! Quickly! Back to the cabin!" Nana Gazelle commanded. "They are close!"

"Who?" Aren asked.

Nana Gazelle, still very quick and light on her feet, took off in a sprint, leaving Aren's question unanswered. Without hesitation, the twins turned on their heels and ran. With every pounding step, the fog that covered the ground swirled around their shoes in a ghostly fury. The sun was still hidden behind the trees, making the trail hard to see. But, none of them needed the light to guide them. They knew the way well. They had traversed it often. The lake was their favorite place to spend their free time, swimming or sitting on The Bench while listening to Nana tell her stories. But, not today. It was not meant to be.

They burst through the cabin door, Nana slamming it

shut, then turning the locks, securing it closed.

"Who is close, Nana?" Aren asked, out of breath.

Before Nana could answer, Alexa asked, "Nana, what is happening? Why are my ears glowing? They itch and are burning!" Alexa was at the small mirror that hung on the wall near the hallway. The tips were bright red, and felt as if they were on fire.

Nana Gazelle hurried to the hall closet, threw open the door, and started shoving things aside. She pulled out a wooden chest and knelt on the floor before it. Chanting a few words while her tiny hands fluttered over the elaborate locks, her magic released the mechanism allowing her to lift the lid.

Aren and Alexa looked at each other, perplexed. Neither of them could remember ever seeing the chest before, and they wondered what was in it that was so important.

"Alexa, the fire that burns your ears is a warning that a threat is near," explained Nana. "It's a trait I did not know you had. Never ignore the burn." The look on her face told Alexa their situation was very serious. "Here, take this." From the chest, she handed Alexa a dagger.

"Nana this is beautiful, but what am I to do with it?" Alexa asked, admiring the glimmering stones encrusted in the hilt, while keeping the blade secured in the sheath.

"Use it if necessary," was all Nana said, glancing at

Alexa's ears. She returned to the chest. With great care she handed Aren a sword. "This is the sword that will save our people. Do not lose it. Do not let it in the hands of evil."

Aren accepted the sword, wondering why she was giving it to him. The thought was lost once he pulled the sword from its scabbard. It was truly a magnificent piece of crafted beauty like none he had ever seen before. Intricate carvings stretched the length of the steel blade, which cast a silvery glow as he held it in front of him. A clear blue crystal entwined within the steel made up the fishtail pummel that extended from the end of the hilt. As he held the sword, an overwhelming feeling of acceptance radiated through him. It felt alive in his hand, as if the sword was a part of him.

"Nana, why are you giving this to me?" Aren asked.

"You are the chosen one. The one who must save our people." She looked again at Alexa's ears. "Attach them to your belts. Now listen carefully. We are all in danger!"

A thunderous bang reverberated against the front door stopping Nana Gazelle short.

"Come out, come out, wherever you are!" A gruff voice taunted. "We know you are in there!"

Bam!

"Xendors!" Nana Gazelle said. Recognizing the voice, she shoved the chest back in the closet. She waved her hands at the wall. An opening to a dark tunnel appeared before them. "Run! To The Bench!" she demanded in a loud whisper, as she pushed Aren and Alexa through the opening with more force than she intended. They both stumbled forward, nearly falling.

Bam!

Without warning, the locks and hinges that held the door in place broke off and flew across the room, colliding into Nana Gazelle. The impact forced her to fall back, away from the tunnel's opening. "Grab the satchel! It will explain mo..." Her words were cut off as the door crashed to the ground. But before the dust settled, Nana had managed to return the wall to its normal state.

Three burly Xendor warriors entered the cabin, stomping on the door. All of them had similar appearances, and looked as if they were cut from the same mold. There was one that Nana Gazelle recognized immediately, the one whose voice was all too familiar to her, Odin. He was big and muscular, with tan skin, black unruly hair, and eyes as foreboding as the abyss. A jagged scar near his left eye made Nana smirk, as it reminded her of how he acquired it; it had been from the dagger that Alexa now possessed. The other two men that flanked Odin were unknown to her. They were shorter, and thinner, but still muscular and evil looking.

"Ah, Gazelle, so it is here that you have been hiding all these years! Very clever of you to hide in the Other World." His black eyes bore into her. "So, where are they?" Odin bellowed.

Nana stood, brushing herself off. "Who might that be?" She asked, mocking him.

"You know good and well who! Now, where are those two wretched children?"

"I know of no such children."

"Of course you do," he said, in a sweetly sarcastic tone. "The children you have been hiding. Where are they?"

Nana Gazelle said, "They are not here you fool! You and your goons are too late!"

He did not believe her. "Search the place!" Odin commanded. “And be on the lookout for that sword!”

The two goons, as Nana thought of them, started ransacking the small living room. Pieces of broken furniture flew about as each object was smashed against the walls, littering the floor with splinters of wood and debris. This was clearly a display of destruction as there was no possible way two teenage kids could hide in the sparsely furnished room.

One of the men barreled past Nana, knocking her into the opposite wall through which she had pushed Aren and Alexa. Her head was very close to the mirror when the other man smashed it with his bare hand, sending shards of glass raining all over her. As he walked past her, he snarled in her face. His breath smelled of rotting teeth, but Nana Gazelle did not flinch, or show any indication that she was intimidated. She stared at him straight in the eyes until he moved on, out of sight.

Nana stole a glance at the wall, and to her dismay she could see Aren and Alexa still there on the opposite side. The twins were looking on in horror at the scene occurring inside the cabin. Aren was searching the wall, trying to find a way through. Even though Nana was upset that they had not gone to The Bench as she had instructed, she was not surprised that they could see through the wall also. Their cries of anguish were unheard as the barrier that separated them proved to be soundproof, except to Nana's ears. It was torturous for her to ignore their pleas, but she knew it was in their best interest. She questioned whether the decision to not teach the kids how to use their powers was the right thing to do. She knew that Aren would fight to the death to defend her and his sister, but it was a risk they could not take. He had to return with the sword to their people. He was the only one who could save them.

She willed herself not to look at them for fear that Odin would figure out where they were. He had captured her for sure, but she would not go willingly. She did not want the children to witness what she was sure was going to be a gruesome scene. She wasn't afraid for herself, she was afraid for the twins and her people.

Odin towered over her, staring down upon the strong willed woman. She was as he remembered her, a fearless elfin, with purplish-grey hair that matched the color of her eyes. Her face bore a few more wrinkles than before, but she was still pretty, in her own way. He admired her tenacity and strength for such a petite and elderly woman. But even so, he had a job to do, and that was to retrieve the sword, and the boy. Capturing Gazelle was a bonus.

"I see you are going to be difficult. If they are here, my men will find them, and it won't be pleasant," Odin threatened, as his men tore apart the kitchen.

There was no doubt in Nana's mind that these men would hurt, or possibly even kill the twins. Without Aren, the sword was useless to their people. Refusing to succumb to Odin's threats, she glared at him as she listened to his men destroy the dining table and chairs. They emptied out the cabinets, throwing everything to the ground. It didn't matter. Nana knew no one would ever be utilizing any of it again.

The two Xendors headed up the stairs and proceeded to annihilate the bedrooms.

"As I said before, they are not here. You and your goons are wasting your time."

"We shall see." His eyes roamed around the room, scrutinizing every crack and crevice.

Nana used this moment to steal a glance at the children who were still behind the wall. While Odin's back was to her, she mouthed to the kids, "RUN!" with a very stern look.

Odin turned in time to see her glaring at the wall.

"Hmmm, you find this wall interesting, do you, Gazelle?" Odin stepped closer, inspecting it.

Alexa's eyes grew wide at the sight of Odin seemingly staring right at them. It was apparent though that he could not see them as they could see him. Alexa took note of Odin's size, noticing that Aren was almost the same height, but not as muscular.

Even though Odin couldn't see him, Aren was steadfast as he glared at Odin's translucent form. He punched at the wall level with Odin's face, but it stood firm leaving Aren with nothing but a throbbing hand.

Alexa grabbed at Aren's arm, tugging at him in an effort to get him to run as Nana had instructed.

With Odin's back to her, Nana looked about for a weapon. The shattered pieces of glass from the mirror were too small to do any good. Near her feet she spied a spindle from the wooden rocking chair. It wasn't much of a weapon, but it would have to do. She crouched down, grabbed the spindle, and with one quick, fluid movement, spun around and whacked Odin in the back of the head.

The force of the blow broke the spindle in half, and caused Odin's head to slam forward into the wall with a sickening crack. Odin staggered backwards, nearly falling. Before he could regain his balance, Nana lunged at him stabbing him in the shoulder. Odin screamed out in pain as its jagged edges penetrated his flesh. Nana pulled back her weapon and struck again, catching him in the right cheek. Blood oozed from his wounds.

Odin flailed his arms, swatting Nana hard, sending her sailing across the room, onto the fallen door. Filled with rage, he pulled out his sword and barreled towards her. He was furious with himself. He knew better than to turn his back on Gazelle. It was no surprise that she still possessed the strength and agility that she had the last time he encountered her. The scar on his face was a constant reminder of their last encounter.

Nana Gazelle struggled to stand as Odin pointed the blade directly at her heart. She finally stood erect before him in defiance, with his sword poking her ribs.

Odin's two sentries charged into the room stopping short, puzzled at the sight before them. They had been making such a racket destroying the upstairs that they did not hear the commotion downstairs. Their confusion dissipated when they saw the blood, and look on Odin's face. It wasn't hard to figure out that Gazelle must have attacked him.

Daring to speak, one of the men declared, "Neither the kids, nor the sword are here!"

A guttural scream erupted from deep within Odin as the fury that burned like boiling lava exploded. Unleashing his wrath upon Nana Gazelle, he plunged his sword into her chest, penetrating her heart.

Chapter Two

Odin pulled his sword from Nana Gazelle, and watched as she crumpled onto the broken door. A gust of wind stirred around Nana's lifeless body lifting her remains as they disintegrated into a dust. The air churned as her ashes swirled and drifted out the open doorway. The three Xendors stood in silence, frozen in time.

While staring at what once was Nana Gazelle drift away, Odin swatted at something tickling his neck. Feeling nothing unusual with his fingers, he realized there was a breeze whipping his hair back and forth. As he turned to look for the source of the draft, he noticed a tunnel through an opening in the wall. He had been so caught up with the scene of Nana Gazelle's death, he did not notice that the wall was no longer there. Once she had died, the magic that held the wall in place vanished, exposing the tunnel. She had not had enough time to place a permanent spell to keep the tunnel hidden before the Xendors crashed through the door.

Odin yelled at his sentries, who were still staring out the doorway, "A tunnel! Go after them! Catch them, and do not let them get away!"

As the two men ran off, Odin noticed the cupboard near the tunnel's entrance that they had missed. He trudged over and flung open the doors. A heap of clothes were piled on top of a wooden box. He pushed the articles aside, uncovering the box. It wasn't just a box, it was a chest! A chest that was just the right length to house a sword! His heart began to pound. Kneeling before it, he pushed up the lid. Empty. Fuming, he smashed the chest closed with his fists.

Odin decided to look around the cabin to see if he could find anything else of importance that may have been missed. He lumbered up the stairs and entered the first room. All it contained was the remains of an armoire that held a few articles of women's clothing, a bed, and several insignificant items. Finding nothing, he went to the next room.

Glancing around at the unfamiliar items, he figured they must belong to a girl. Initially, he found nothing of interest and was about to leave the room until he spied a broken bow. "Well, well, what do you know? The little lady knows a bit about archery," he said, while inspecting its quality and craftsmanship. He tossed it to the floor, stepping towards the door. A loud crunch under his boot caught his attention. He kicked at the object and then realized its importance. Broken glass surrounded by a gold frame held a picture of two people. He picked it up recognizing some of the features of the two, but not the people themselves. The picture was of a young girl and boy.

They were standing in a lake, completely wet as if they had just gone under the water. The two were hugging each other in a playful way, grinning from ear to ear. There was no mistaking that these were the children of Yasmin and Erik Rainz, for they had their mother's black hair, and their father's bright blue eyes. The girl's facial features resembled that of their mother, and the boy's of their father. He removed the picture and pocketed it, tossing the frame across the room. He then moved on to the next room.

Stepping into Aren's room, the first thing Odin saw was a map that was torn in half, but still hanging on the wall from its corners. Pieces of debris snapped as he trampled across the room to get to it. He smoothed the two pieces up with his hands and held them together. There were no words on the map, just images. He recognized the terrain. This was a map of the Vesterra region. There was a red 'X' that marked a spot over a waterfall that he knew to be Rheyaros. Far to the left of Rheyaros was the image of two unique mountain peaks, which depicted Pellyn. This was where the elfin clan had resided before poison plagued the river that flowed through their village, forcing them to leave. Beyond Pellyn and Rheyaros, a black peak protruded from dismal clouds depicting Brunridge, Odin’s home. He did not need to study the map for he knew the area well.

As he exited the room, the corners of his lips curled, marveling at the amount of destruction his two sentries had accomplished in such a short period of time. As unnecessary as it was, he was pretty sure they had broken nearly every item in the home.

Bounding down the stairs en route to the tunnel he heard a loud rumbling noise, and then the stairs started to shake beneath him. He lost his balance, tumbling to the bottom.

Chapter Three

The rocky walls of the tunnel illuminated around them, and a short distance in front of them, directing the way. Beyond the light was completely dark, making it impossible to tell which way the tunnel would turn. The passageway was narrow and barely wide enough for Aren's shoulders to fit. In some areas, the ceiling was so low he had to duck. Alexa, being petite, had no problem maneuvering through the tunnel.

They did not go far before Aren stopped. "I can't, I can't leave her behind. We need to go back," he said.

Alexa hated to leave Nana Gazelle behind, but she knew it was what they had to do. She had tugged at Aren's arms as he stood strong staring down Odin through the wall. "Come on Aren, we have to go," Alexa had pleaded. "Nana wouldn't order us to go if it wasn't supposed to be this way. We have to go!"

Reluctantly, Aren had given in to his sister's demands and turned to follow her through the tunnel. He knew she was right, but his heart ached at the thought of leaving Nana. And now, his conscience was telling him to turn back.

But then, they heard yelling in the passageway from which they had just come. It was the Xendors that had been tearing apart their cabin! They were running in the dark trying not to crash into the walls. Because the tunnel did not light up for them as it did for Aren and Alexa, it was more difficult for them to navigate their course.

In the distance ahead, the Xendors could see two silhouettes, and assumed it was the two kids they were after. Using their hands as guides along the walls, they continued their pursuit through the hindering darkness, battering their bodies along the way.

Seeing the Xendors approaching, the twins turned in the opposite direction and ran. The tunnel took a slight turn to the right, then widened into a spacious cavern. Brilliant crystals, glimmering in a kaleidoscope of color, covered the entire ceiling. The sight was magical, and they tried to take it all in without slowing down. Nearing the end, Aren risked peering over his shoulder to check the status of the Xendors. As his head was turned, he did not notice, until it was too late, that Alexa had stopped in front of him. Like a bulldozer, he plowed into her sending her soaring through the air. She landed hard, banging her chin on the ground, and sliding on her stomach, until she came to an abrupt stop against the wall.

"Oh my gosh! Alexa! I'm sorry! Are you okay?" He ran to her side.

She lay against the wall with her eyes closed, trying to suck in air. The blow had knocked the wind out of her.

He put his hands out to touch her but was afraid to move her, unsure if she was severely hurt. He wondered what had caused her to stop without warning.

As if reading his mind, his question was answered as she managed to lift her arm and point up towards the ceiling. She struggled to speak, but with great effort she managed to gasp, "The ... satchel ... up ... there."

He looked up to where she was pointing and saw the satchel hanging high from a hook on the side of the wall. A lone crystal hung above it showering it with light, as if it was an artifact on display. In the seconds that he had turned his head to look for the Xendors, he had missed seeing it, and was thankful that Alexa had been paying attention.

"I'll get it," he said with a hint of guilt in his voice.

The brown leather satchel, old and worn but still in good condition, hung from a gnarled hook. Aren reached up and removed the satchel, noticing its weight. He draped it across his shoulders so it hung from the opposite side as the sword. He was about to turn away, but then noticed that the hook started to slowly retreat towards a hole in the wall from which it appeared to have been carved. As it moved upward, the light from the crystal started to dim. *Interesting,* he thought. Even though he could hear the Xendors entering the cavern, Aren could not stop watching as the hook made its final decent into the hole. It fit perfectly, like a puzzle piece. *Click*. The light from the crystal disappeared. Then there was a loud rumbling sound, and the ground started to shake. It felt like an earthquake! Rocks and crystals started to fall from the ceiling, exploding on impact with the ground.

Aren tried to keep his balance as he scrambled towards Alexa, who was attempting to stand. Her knees buckled, and she fell as the ground shook beneath her. Aren rushed to her, grabbing her under her arms, and lifting her to her feet.

"We need to get out of here!" he yelled. "Can you manage?"

"Yes, I think so," she said. Her breathing had returned to normal, but her body felt beaten. She trudged forward on wobbly legs as Aren continued to hold onto her with one hand under her arm.

Their adrenaline spiked seeing that the Xendors were now half way through the cavern. They had no idea how much farther they had to go, but were glad to be turning a corner, out of the Xendors' sight. Although the light still shown in front of, and around them, the tunnel was starting to fill with dust and debris, clouding the air and irritating their eyes.

Through the rumbling of the collapsing tunnel, they heard the Xendors screaming as tons of rocks and crystals crashed down upon them. Hearing their cries encouraged Aren and Alexa to quicken their pace.

Without warning, the light dissipated and for a

moment they were running in complete darkness. Up ahead, Aren noticed a wall fragmented with small specks of light peeking through. He hoped it was an exit, but he couldn't really tell through the dust. He decided to charge at it anyway. Pulling Alexa behind him, he plowed forward. The barrier exploded on impact. They tripped, and tumbled on the ground, temporarily blinded by the brightness of daylight.

Aren stood, rubbing the dust from his eyes. He looked back at the tunnel. A parting of branches from their exit through the dense thicket no longer camouflaged its opening. He reached down and helped Alexa up. They looked around to gather their bearings, and realized they were just off the trail near Ice Lake. Puzzled, Aren turned back to study the tunnel. He felt a bit daft for never noticing it before.

Then Alexa said, "Weird, I've never knew there was a tunnel."

"Me either." Even though Alexa's confession made Aren feel slightly better about himself, he vowed to be more aware of his surroundings from now on.

They had just finished brushing the dirt and leaves from their bodies, when, without warning, a huge plume of dust billowed out of the tunnel spewing a colossal cloud of residue through the bushes. The entire tunnel had just collapsed.

Aren and Alexa stepped back, shielding their eyes, as they were showered with bits of debris. Once the dust had settled, and they were able to peer at what used to be the tunnel, they both knew that there was no way anyone who was still inside could have survived. They were thankful they had not met the same fate as the Xendors.

Chapter Four

Alexa sat on The Bench with her feet tucked under her. Her body ached from Aren slamming into her, and then striking the wall. Aside from the abrasion on her chin and being sore, she seemed to physically be okay, nothing appeared to be broken. What she knew would not mend was her aching heart. Tears were streaming from her eyes while haunting thoughts of what might have happened to Nana Gazelle invaded her mind. "Why did Nana want us to come to The Bench?" Alexa asked, not sure if Aren was listening. "Maybe she plans on meeting us here." Deep inside she knew that Nana was not going to show. Through tear blurred vision, she sat and watched her brother pace back and forth in front of her.

Aren was feeling very irritated with himself for having left Nana Gazelle, and wished he could have found a way through the wall. He, too, wondered why Nana wanted them to run to The Bench. As if his hand held an answer, he stared at it as he flexed it open and closed, trying to relieve some of the soreness from having punched the wall. He kept thinking there was more that he could have done than just run, *but what?* He felt like a coward for not being able to defend Nana. With that thought, his hand unconsciously went to the hilt of the sword. He looked down at it thinking he could have used it to kill those jerks that ruined their lives. Looking at his sister, he noticed her ears were no longer red. It must mean the Xendors were gone, at least two of them were most likely dead.

"I could see Nana through the wall," Alexa said, wiping away her tears. "It was a bit fuzzy, but I could see her."

"I could see her also," Aren added. "I got a pretty good look at that Xendor, too. I won't be forgetting what he looked like." He rubbed the hilt of the sword.

"We must have some powers like Nana's if we were able to see through the wall. I wonder why we've never noticed any powers before?"

"Good question. My guess is it's because we have never needed to use them before." He sat down next to Alexa, feeling deflated.

She wrapped her arms around his chest and rested her head on his shoulder.

Aren bent forward with his elbows resting on his knees, and his face buried in his hands. "I'm sorry I crashed into you. And, I'm sorry ... whoa!"

Before either of them could react, the granite seat of The Bench pulled out from under them, then tilted, dropping the twins into a void between the two boulders. As quickly as it opened, the seat closed once it deposited the two.

They both screamed as they fell through the blackness. There was nothing to reach for. Nothing to grab onto. Nothing to stop them from falling. Just air. The farther they fell, the cooler the air became. They were falling so fast they could hardly catch their breaths. Then, the downward drop came to an abrupt stop. They were suspended in midair, floating in nothingness.

"What's happening, Aren?" Alexa shrieked.

He did not know, but before he could answer a misty wind-spun vortex began to form, filling the void. Its pull became powerful, sucking hard at them. It swallowed them with a force that gripped hard at their bodies. They were jerked through the cloudy portal; first their heads, then their shoulders, all the way down to their feet. They were squeezed through with pressure hugging them so tightly they thought they would be squished to death like a bug. Alexa tried to scream, but there was no sound.

One after the other they popped out of the portal and were sent sliding through a lava rock tube. Splashes of white lights lit up the chute as they sped through its many twists and turns. They slid with such incredible speed that the light soon became one long thin beam radiating above them.

Alexa tried to reach above her head to grab hold of Aren's legs, but he was too far away. She screamed as jet streams of air propelled her forward. A short drop sent her airborne, but did nothing to slow her velocity as gravity pulled her spiraling through the chute. The heels of her boots dug into the ground as she was spit out into the open. Her boots pushed up a mound of mud-caked moss as she slid on her back across the damp ground. She came to a stop none too soon, just feet from a cliff high above a huge valley. A flood of relief washed over her as she took in the view. It was amazing. She had never seen anything like it.

While admiring a cascading waterfall in the far distance, something slammed into her lower back, pitching her towards the edge of the cliff. She could not stop herself and screamed at the realization that she would soon be careening over the precipice to her death. In a split second, she thought to pull out the dagger and drive it into the ground. She held on to the hilt with all her might as her lower body slid over the edge. Her arm stretched its full length above her head, nearly yanking her shoulder out of its socket. She fought to hold on as her legs dangled precariously over the cliff. With her face buried into the ground, she tried to pull herself to safety. The dagger loosened. Panic engulfed her. She yelled to Aren for help. The dagger continued to slip.

Aren grabbed a fistful of Alexa's hair just as the dagger broke free. He heaved her toward him knocking himself backwards with Alexa landing on top of him. Holding her firmly against his chest, he breathed hard. The thought of virtually sending his sister toppling to her death frightened him. He had shot out of the tube unable to stop himself from ramming into her.

He did not realize how tightly he was clutching her until she started to squirm under his grip. Her hair unraveled from his fingers as he loosened his hold.

With what strength she had left, Alexa pushed herself away, gasping for air. As soon as she regained her ability to breathe, she forced herself to stand. She glared at him, and shouted, "Oh my gosh, Aren! Not only did you try to kill me earlier in the tunnel by slamming into me, and knocking the wind out of me, scraping up my face," she jutted out her chin, pointing towards the abrasion, "but, you also tried to kill me by kicking me in the butt, nearly sending me over the edge of the cliff!"

His eyes followed her finger as she pointed out over the cliff. His stomach turned at the thought.

"And then! And then you try to suffocate me by smothering me against you!" she yelled, with words spewing out of her mouth so quickly it surprised even her. "Did I do something to piss you off?" she concluded. Then she kicked him in his side.

He accepted the kick as well deserved punishment. "I'm really sorry Lex. It was an accident. I couldn't stop myself."

"You are no longer allowed to call me Lex! It's Alexa!" she retorted, as she bent down to pick up the mud covered dagger. "Now get up and let's figure out where we are, and what we're doing here before something else happens!" she demanded, while wiping the blade onto her already mud and moss stained pants.

Chapter Five

"Where the heck are we anyway?" Alexa asked.

They surveyed the area from the plateau that overlooked a huge valley. Aren recognized it as the same that was on the map he had hanging on his bedroom wall.

"We're in Vesterra," he said. "Look there." Aren pointed to a horseshoe shaped waterfall that cascaded from the top of a mountain, seemingly into the trees. "That is Rheyaros. That is where our elfin family live now, according to Nana. And way over there, that is Pellyn," he said, pointing to the two pinnacle shaped mountains. The waterfall that flowed between them was not visible from where they stood, but there was no mistaking the jagged crowns that shaped the peaks of Pellyn. A river that traveled through the dense forest of the valley on either side of a huge lake was what separated Rheyaros from Pellyn. "See where that ugly gray cloud is covering that dark mountain? That is Brunridge."

Alexa followed his gaze across the valley from one point to the other. A flood of emotions filled her as the realization of where they were settled in. "Wow! Okay," was all she could think to say. Then, after a few minutes of gazing at the wondrous view, she suggested, "I suppose we should look in the satchel and see if it explains more like Nana had said. Then maybe we should head towards Rheyaros and see if we can find our parents."

"Agreed," said Aren. "I'm hoping the satchel has something in it to eat, because I'm starving."

They sat cross-legged, facing each other, eager to reveal the contents of the satchel. Aren laid it in his lap and untied the strings that held the flap in place. As he lifted the flap they both leaned forward to peer inside, knocking their foreheads together. Pulling back, they gave each other a look as Alexa rubbed at her forehead. She decided to sit back and watch Aren retrieve its contents.

He pulled out a very old looking leather bound book filled with yellowing pages of parchment. The book, although not very thick, was rather heavy for its size. Opening it he found the first two pages were covered with a detailed map of Vesterra. The map was condensed, and hard to read. Aren studied it for a moment noticing there were several trails that curved about the entire region. He turned the page to find the familiar scrawl of Nana's handwriting. A pang of sadness filled his heart at the sight of her script. After a brief moment, Aren began to read out loud:

Dear Aren and Alexa, if you are reading this then I am already dead. Do not fret over me for I have fulfilled my destiny in life, and am content with the life I have lived. Had it not been for you two, my time may have ended years ago. Thank you for allowing me the joy of spending my final years with the two most remarkable children I have ever known. Now enough of the sappiness (Alexa dry those tears).

At those words, Alexa let out a strained chuckle and wiped at the tears streaming down her face. It was so like Nana to not dwell on emotions. She always felt they got in the way of thinking and acting rationally. Alexa knew Nana was right, if she dwelled on the fact that Nana was dead, she would succumb to grief and not be able to function. She could grieve later when she was safe with their people. For now, she needed to control her emotions and concentrate on finding her way home.

Aren reached up and tenderly placed his hand on his sister's cheek, wiping with his thumb at a final tear that leaked from her eye. He knew he needed to be strong for Alexa's sake. He tried to hide the anger that was welling up inside him over Nana's death. As soon as Alexa nodded at him to let him know she was okay, he proceeded with reading.

By now you have probably noticed that you are in Vesterra. I had hoped to be able to return with you, but that was not meant to be. You are probably wondering why The Bench had never opened up before; when the satchel was removed from the hook, and the hook was locked back in its original place, it triggered The Bench to open once enough pressure, the combined calculated weight of the two of you, was placed on it. Clever, huh?

I can guide you off the mountain, but from there you will need to find the safest way to Rheyaros on your own. There is a path that leads down the mountain, behind the rock that sits next to the opening of the tunnel you arrived from.

They both turned to looked at the rock.

Follow the path, which will end short of the bottom, and walk straight through the flora for thirty yards or so. Be wary of the spur bushes! They are very poisonous! You will know one the moment you see it; the thorns are huge! Once through, find the tree with an arrow carved in it approximately ten feet from the ground. Walk in the direction the arrow points until you find the next tree, and so on. There will be eight marked trees, about fifty yards apart (yes, Aren, that is the distance of half a football field).

This caused Aren to chuckle. Not only did he like to play football, but he was also an avid fan of the sport.

Just past the eighth tree will be a path. To the right will lead you in the direction of Rheyaros.

In the satchel you will find a tube filled with wafers. Each wafer is the equivalent of a full meal and will fill your bellies for hours. Eat sparingly, but do not go hungry for you need to maintain your strength. There should be plenty to sustain you until you reach home.

There isn't enough time for you two to sit and dawdle by reading the entire journal. Read it along the way as time allows. Eat, then go find your way off the mountain.

Aren peeked inside the satchel and noticed the tube. Holding it up in front of them he looked at it wondering how 'full meals' could fit inside this six-inch long tube. Twisting off the cap, he tipped it upside down, dropping a couple wafers onto his palm. They were an avocado green color, thin and flat, about the size of quarter.

"Eww, I hope those aren't moldy," said Alexa, as she crinkled her nose at the sight of them.

Aren brought one to his nose. "They don't smell like anything. Do you want one?"

"You first."

“Figures, I always have to be the guinea pig,” he said. Without further hesitation he popped one in his mouth. He immediately started gagging, and choking, grabbing at his throat with both hands.

Alexa screamed as she reached for her brother, "Aren! Oh my gosh, spit it out! Spit it out! You're going to die!"

Just then Aren fell to the ground and started laughing, while chewing. He was laughing so hard he couldn't stop.

"Aren! What the heck! What is so funny? I thought you were dying!" Alexa screamed at him.

"You should have seen your face! It was classic!" he

managed to say, between fits of laughter.

"That's not funny!" Alexa protested. She glared at him with her arms crossed against her chest.

"Okay, okay, I'm sorry. I just couldn't help myself," he said. "But that was hecka funny. Here, you should try one. They really are good."

If she wasn't so hungry she would have refused his offer out of stubbornness. Instead, she snatched the wafer out of his hand. Chewing gingerly, she savored the flavors as the taste of roast beef, garlic mashed potatoes with gravy, peppered green beans, and finally apple pie burst in her mouth. "Wow, that really was good. And, I feel full too, as if I just ate a whole meal."

"Nana sure does know how to serve up a meal, doesn't she? Even in a little wafer," Aren said. Feeling satiated, he screwed the cap back on the tube and returned it to the satchel.

"I guess we should be going," said Alexa.

They headed toward the rock that marked the beginning of the path. It was a narrow dirt trail that snaked down the mountain side. The air cooled slightly under the shade from the trees, making it the perfect temperature. The trees were tall and leafy, and emitted a slight minty aroma that gave the forest a fresh clean smell. The trunks of the trees were covered in moss, as was the ground surrounding them. Several streams of water trickled across the dirt path giving off a wet earthy scent.

They walked in silence nearly half way down the mountain before Aren spoke. "I just thought of something."

"Oh no, that could be dangerous. You thinking!" Alexa teased.

"Very funny. What I was thinking was that I don't remember seeing your ears go red as you were dangling over the edge of the cliff," Aren said. "When they glowed before, I thought that meant your life was in danger because the Xendors were after us. But, they weren't red when you were about to go over the cliff, and your life was definitely in danger then."

Alexa touched her ears at the reminder. He was right, she didn't feel them burning as she was dangling over the cliff. She's not sure she would have being as scared as she was, but maybe. "Hmm, that is rather curious. Are you sure?"

"I'm sure."

She thought about it for a few minutes, then suggested, "Maybe they only turn red when it means that an enemy force is nearby that wants to endanger my life. There was no enemy there at the time. Well, depending on how you look at it, you did try to kill me."

"Oh stop, I would die for you, and you know it."

"Okay, I'm just teasing. Anyway, maybe because you aren't trying to kill me on purpose, and you aren't my true enemy, is why they didn't glow," she reasoned. “Nana did say the fire that burns my ears is a sign that an evil threat is near.”

He pondered this, then said, "That sounds logical since your ears have never glowed before, as far back as I can remember. You don't have any enemies that want to hurt or kill you at school or anything. So maybe that's it."

Alexa said, "If they are going to burn, this will be the place it will happen."

Chapter Six

Waiting was the worst part. Knots twisted in Odin's stomach as he reflected on the demoralizing sense of failure that consumed him once he realized the kids had escaped. Now he stood alone in the dimly lit chamber, with nothing else to think about except for how Mara might react to the news. He thought back to when the quaking had started that caused him to fall down the stairs. When he had finally reached the tunnel, he stopped short of its entrance as it collapsed before him. The sound of grown men screaming echoed in his ears. It was at that moment that he knew his sentries were doomed. Dust had blown all around him, causing him to cough violently. He had run outside, breathing in huge gulps of fresh air. Knowing he had to report back to Mara and explain to her that the kids had escaped, and the sword was gone, caused his bowels to loosen. At least he accomplished one thing that he was sure would please her, he had killed Gazelle.

As Mara walked in, her eyes caught Odin's as they lingered on the long black dress that hugged her slender, yet shapely frame. With every graceful step, her legs pushed against her dress exposing the red pleats that were otherwise hidden. She carefully placed a candle on the table next to her high back chair. She decided not to sit. Standing upon the dais, as her sentry stood below, made her feel domineering. The fingers of light that streamed through the narrow windows behind her highlighted her hair, giving the illusion that her wavy red locks were on fire. Her naturally pale skin looked bruised in the shadows. She liked it that way. It gave her a frightening look that dared people to challenge her.

"What do you mean you found them but they got away?" Mara screamed.

"It was Gazelle. We found her in the Other World, living in a cabin in the woods where she had apparently been raising the kids this whole time," Odin explained. "By the time we got to her cabin, the kids had escaped through a hidden tunnel that materialized once I killed her."

"You killed Gazelle?" Mara asked. Her crimson red lips curved into a devious smile. Her gaze fell upon the gash on his cheek, then moved to the abrasion on his forehead. By the extent of his injuries she surmised that Gazelle must have put up a pretty good fight.

"Yes, she is dead for sure," Odin said, with more elation and pride than he felt. "But, I do not know how they knew we were coming," he reflected, while biting at his lip as he stared down at the stone flooring.

"You must have made your presence known somehow."

"We were very cautious and very stealth." His eyes

met hers.

Her eyebrows rose as she glared at him. She did not believe they were as prudent as he thought. How else would Gazelle have known they were coming?

"My two sentries perished in the tunnel, chasing after the kids. It collapsed on them. They were good men," he said.

"There are others," she said, waving her hand in a gesture that showed how irrelevant the lives of the sentries were to her. There were plenty of men out there eager to serve under one of the most powerful women in the region, one who would surely control the entire region within a matter of days. *If I could just get my hands on that sword,* she thought.

"Those two were the best that ever served," he said.

Her green eyes blazed, showing her annoyance at his sentimentality towards his sentries.

A wave of heat flushed his cheeks when he saw the way she was looking at him. Embarrassed, he quickly changed the subject, for he did not want her to think of him as weak. He stood tall and puffed out his chest. "Anyway, I'm sure the children are here in the Vesterra region. I scoured the area of their cabin but they were nowhere to be found. They have the sword, I'm sure of that also."

"How do you know they have the sword?"

"I found an empty chest that appeared to have once

held the sword," he explained. Then he pulled out the photograph of the two kids that he carried inside a pocket. "I also found this." Odin knew bringing items back from the Other World to this world was forbidden, but this one little item was small, and could prove very important.

Her eyes slowly moved from Odin to the photograph that she now held in her hand. Studying it with intense interest, she knew immediately the two pictured were Aren and Alexa. The resemblance of both their mother and father was very evident. “Rather good looking kids,” she said. “It runs in the family.”

He gave her time to study the photograph before speaking. "They must be here to return the sword to their people before the night of the Skylar Moon, which will be appearing soon."

"I am very well aware of when the Skylar Moon will appear," her words dripped with sarcasm. She paused for a few moments before speaking again, staring him down with the purpose of making him feel uncomfortable. "Select yourself two new sentries. Ones that won't get themselves killed chasing after two children. Then find them! Find those two beastly children before the night of the Skylar Moon! Kill them if you have to, just bring me that sword!" she commanded, with a tone of finality.

"Yes, my Lady Mara," he said, as he bowed to her. Then he turned on his heels and left. Knowing her stare was upon him, he walked with an air of confidence that betrayed his true feelings. He was annoyed with himself, and inwardly felt ashamed of the behavior he had exhibited in front of her. How she thought of him as a man, as a warrior, was more important to him than anything else.

Lowering herself into her chair, she watched Odin walk away. Her mind swirled trying to decipher her feelings towards him. He was a fine specimen, fearsome, strong and intelligent. All the qualities she thought she might desire in a man. She admired him, but did she love him? How could she? Was she even capable of loving anyone? The only person she knew she had ever loved was her father, but he was dead now. What she felt for Odin was very different than what she had felt for her father. Putting a label on her feelings was something she tried to avoid. Right now, she had other things to worry about.

Chapter Seven

They finally reached the end of the path after what seemed like hours. To their dismay, they came upon a wall of spur bushes.

Aren stared at them with a concerned look on his face, and asked rhetorically, "How the heck are we supposed to walk through those things?" He threw his arms in the air. "There is no way I'm stepping a foot in these bushes. Remember when Nana told us about the guy who was chasing her, and a thorn poked him in just the right spot? Then he doubled over in pain and collapsed face first into the bushes. When his cohorts finally pulled him out, he was unconscious with thorns sticking out all over his body. He lost his manhood that day. That is so not going to happen to me! No way!"

Alexa rolled her eyes, and chuckled at the memory. Nana had laughed hysterically as she told the story. "Served the goon right for chasing after me!" she remembered Nana saying. Nana called all bad guys goons.

"Don't panic just yet. Let's look around for another route," Alexa suggested, knowing Nana would not send them through such a dangerous path.

"But, Nana wrote to walk 'straight', and that's what

we should do, or we'll probably go the wrong way."

"Well, look," Alexa said, pointing to the ground. "The trail appears to end, but there is still a small strip of it that is continuing, and turns at an angle right there. It looks as if the bushes may have grown over the path here." She moved her finger in the direction the path would have gone if the bushes weren't covering it. "That is probably the way we are supposed to go."

"Sounds good to me!" Aren agreed, noticing that there were no spur bushes in the immediate area where she was pointing. He spied ahead before starting out and noticed a line of different plants that didn't appear to be dangerous. But just one step in the wrong direction, and the spur bushes were everywhere. "We need to be really careful."

"Okay. You go first since you're taller, and can see farther ahead. I'll follow you," Alexa smirked.

"Whatever. If one of those thorns pokes me, just think how much trouble you could be in. You're not strong enough to carry me out all by yourself. Then, you would be all alone, here, in this strangely familiar place," he said, waving his hands about.

"It's not me who would be in trouble. It's you. You would be *stuck* here," she said, emphasizing the word. "Literally!" She laughed at her own joke.

"Ha ha, very funny. Stay close," Aren said.

The plants were fragrant with a familiar fresh scent

that neither one of them could place. They were tall and dense, making it difficult to walk through. A tangle of leafy vines covered the entire ground.

With every step Aren took, he breathed a sigh of relief that he was a bit closer to the end without being poked by a thorn. The thought of falling into a spur bush made his stomach turn. Aren was careful to lift his feet high so his shoes would not get tangled up in a vine.

Alexa followed in his footsteps, with one hand stretched out touching his shirt. They were nearly half way across when her foot got caught in the vines. She fell forward into Aren's back as he was taking a step, knocking him off balance. He twisted sideways, rooting his feet to the ground. He reached back, grabbing for Alexa. She slipped through his grasp, pushing against the back of his legs. His knees buckled with the pressure. He flailed his arms trying to regain his balance as his body bent forward awkwardly. To his dismay, he found himself leaning dangerously close to a lone spur bush. Somehow, he managed to steady his bent body, and froze like a mannequin. His face was inches from a thorn. Panic started to rise in him as the thorn seemed to slowly stretch towards his nose, threatening to pierce it. Staring at the thorn, he realized that if Alexa moved even the slightest bit, he would face-plant it right into the spur bush!

He screamed to Alexa, "Don't move!"

Alexa stiffened. Her head was covered in leaves, and

was faced in the opposite direction. "Why?" she asked, frightened at the tone of his voice.

He said, "Don't move. Please. Just give me a second to move first. There are thorns threatening my life."

"What?" Perplexed, she wasn't sure how serious the situation was, until she gradually turned her head in his direction to see what was happening. Appreciating the predicament he was in, she laid motionless. For some reason though, she found it comical to see such fear on Aren's face. A laugh threatened to erupt as she thought about what must be racing through his mind about losing his manhood, even though it was his nose that was in danger.

Keeping his arms stretched out for leverage, Aren slowly rose, straightening his body. Before moving, he looked around trying to figure out his next step. To his horror, he noticed that the thorn on the bush was now level with the same area of his body that the goon was robbed of. He decided he needed to get out of there and fast! Side-stepping away from the bush, he was careful not to trample his sister. He figured if he stepped on her, well, she would heal, eventually. When he was a safe distance, he turned, weak-kneed, and looked down at Alexa. She still laid motionless, but sported a huge smile on her face.

"What's so funny?" he asked.

"Oh, nothing," she said, sucking in her cheeks to hide her smile. "Um, are you going to help me up? Or did that bush steal away your gentlemanly manners?" She giggled as she said it.

"You're such a comedian, Alexa." He was annoyed that she was making fun of him. "Are you hurt?"

"No, I think I'm okay. My foot is just stuck in these vines. I don't think it's sprained, though."

"Well, you're going to have to try to get your foot out by yourself, because I'm not going to risk going near that spur bush to help you."

"Sissy," she said, under her breath, smirking as she sat up twisting her leg around. Her foot moved easily under the vines, but it still took her several seconds to free herself. She turned onto her knees, readying herself to push up into a standing position. Out of the corner of her eye, she could see one of the thorns from the spur bush pointing right at her. Looking at it, she decided her brother wasn't such a sissy after all. The thorn appeared to be stretching towards her, and looked big enough to take down a rhinoceros. If she lost her balance while trying to stand up where she was, she would fall right into that spur bush. *No thank you!* She decided to crawl forward a few feet on her hands and knees before trying to stand. Moving quickly, she reached Aren's feet, and then reached for his outstretched hand, allowing him to help her up.

"What?" she asked, noticing the mocking look he was giving her.

"Sissy, huh? Come on, let's get out of here."

They walked on in silence, without further incident until they were free of the bushes. The thirty yard trek seemed more like a mile and took them a lot longer than they expected. Aren breathed a deep sigh of relief as he took his first step out of the lethal vegetation.

Alexa noticed the tree first. "Look. Up there. That tree has the arrow carved into it. Looks as if we need to go that way."

They headed in the direction the arrow pointed and soon found the next tree, and then the next. The marked trees proved relatively easy to find in the grove of giant evergreens. Walking on the powdery dirt that carpeted the ground was effortless. The area was free of shrubs and other plants, contributing to its untouched beauty. Their only obstacles were the gnarled tree roots that protruded from the soil. The entire area was under an umbrella of shade as the branches of one tree stretched out as if reaching for the branches of its neighboring tree, blocking out the sun.

"Some of these trees are rather strange looking," Alexa commented, as she inspected the wide branch of an enormous tree she was walking under.

"How so?"

"Look at those bottom branches. The way they are shaped looks as if you could sit in them, or sleep in them. Kind of like a hammock."

"Ha! You're right. When we get to the trail, maybe we should take a break in one of those trees before we continue on," suggested Aren.

"Maybe we should consider calling it a night before we continue on. It's starting to get dark," Alexa noted.

"That's a good idea. We'll try to find one of those trees with the hammock branches closer to the trail. That way in the morning we can jump on the trail and go."

They reached the eighth tree with the symbol on it, and then found the trail that would lead them towards Rheyaros. The gravely surface of the trail made a crunching sound under their shoes as they stepped. The change of scenery was drastic. The grove of trees merged into an area crowded with rocks and boulders with thin saplings growing sparsely between the crags.

Alexa noticed a small rock that looked a bit out of place a few feet in front of her. She took a few bouncing steps towards it, swung her leg back, and then gave it a kick. It flew through the air making a horrible screeching sound. The noise stopped abruptly as the rock hit a boulder, then it landed on the ground with a thud.

Alexa gasped, as her hands flew to her mouth. "Oh my gosh! I don't think that was a rock!" she exclaimed.

Aren stood with his mouth agape, as Alexa ran to the object. A soft moaning sound emitted from it. With trembling hands, Alexa scooped up the little creature that, upon closer inspection, didn't look like a rock at all. It was a wispy ball of fluffy grey fur. Sticking out of the fur were two thin orange legs, each of which sported a foot, with four itty-bitty toes. With two fingers, she gently stroked what she thought might be the head, opposite the feet. Two round blue eyes popped open, rolled around, and then closed again. Alexa cooed at the little critter, whispering softly to it, "I'm so sorry little guy. I thought you were a rock. Please don't die. I didn't mean to hurt you." She continued to stroke it as Aren looked over her shoulder.

Its eyes fluttered open again, and blinked several times. As they focused on Alexa's face, they widened in fear. The creature started to shake. It popped up, righted itself, and landed on its feet in Alexa's palm. It rolled itself into a ball, tucking its feet inside its fur, making itself look like rock.

"Oh my. I think its scared!" Alexa said.

"It's a cute little thing. What do you suppose it is?" Aren asked.

"It's a pinquist," she said, as if he should have known. "Nana said that these little things are thieves. But I don't see how they could be, they are so dang cute, and tiny. What could they possibly steal, and where would they put it?" She asked, not really expecting an answer. "I want to keep it. It's so cute."

Aren raised an eyebrow at the thought of having a pet while trying to find their way to Rheyaros. "Do you really think that's such a good idea. I mean, we don't even know anything about them. What do they eat? What are its needs?"

"Seriously, Aren. Don't start getting all logical on me now. It will be fine. Besides, I read somewhere that pets can provide comfort to people in times of need, such as in our time of grieving," Alexa pouted as she said it.

"Oh, I see how you're going to be. Use Nana's death to acquire a pet! A rodent at that!"

Alexa's lips started to tremble at his harsh words, and tears started streaming from her eyes.

"Aw, come on Lex. I didn't mean it. If you want to keep it, I'm sure it will be fine," he said, giving in as he grabbed his sister and embraced her affectionately. "How much trouble could a little pinquist be anyway?"

She wiped away the tears, then nuzzled the little fur-ball against her cheek. "Thank you," she said to Aren. "It's already stolen my heart! The little thief!"

It opened its eyes and blinked at her. It shook its body causing the fur to puff out, then started purring softly like a kitten.

Aren laughed at the blissful irony of the situation. "I suppose you should name it if you are going to keep it."

"Hmm. I'll have to think on that one. Do you have any suggestions?"

"Hmm, Bandit would be kind of cute. I guess. If

you're looking for cute. Since he stole your heart and all."

"Oh Aren, that is perfect! I love it! Bandit it is!" she announced, while holding it high up in the air, as if christening the little critter.

"Okay, now that that's settled, let's get back to the trees and find a place to stay for the night."

They found the perfect tree with wide scooping branches within sight of the trail. The branches were a little too high for Aren to jump up and reach so Alexa gave him a boost by entwining her fingers together and then pushing him up by his foot. He grabbed onto the branch and pulled himself up.

Alexa tucked Bandit securely away inside her shirt pocket, and grabbed onto Aren's outstretched hand. She knew she didn't need his help to climb the tree, but she didn't want to make her brother feel bad since he couldn't climb it without her help.

Once settled on the branch, Aren asked, "Are you hungry?"

"No, not really. I'm good until morning. That wafer really filled me up."

"Okay. I can wait until morning also," he said. "I'd like to read a little bit more of Nana's journal, but it's already too dark."

"We'll read it tomorrow," she said. "I'll take that branch over there, and you can sleep on this one." She climbed across to the next branch. It was a bit narrower, the right size for her. She was able to lay lengthwise along the branch as it hugged her on both sides. She retrieved Bandit from her pocket and laid the ball of fur on her chest.

Bandit turned in circles looking around. He took a few slow steps towards Alexa's tummy eyeing the dagger that rested at her side. Ambling back and forth, he slowly inched his way towards the dagger.

Alexa looked on with amusement, wondering what he was going to do once he finally made his way to it. As he approached the dagger, he appeared to sniff at it, although his nose was hidden from view through all the fur. Bandit hopped on the hilt, then hopped right back off. After staring at it for a few more seconds, he lost all interest, and walked back to Alexa's chest. He turned a full circle, curled his feet under his fur, and then balled up. Once he was settled, he opened his eyes, and looked at Alexa with a calm gentleness.

Alexa began stroking his soft fur and noticed his eyes start to droop, and then close, as he began to purr. With Bandit asleep, she decided to take a closer look at the dagger. Pointing the blade towards the night sky, she admired the jewels that adorned the hilt. The stones on one side appeared to be the mirror image of the ones on the other side. She turned it back and forth in her hand thinking the two sides were twins of each other, like her and Aren. Except, on one side there was one extra emerald that laid at the base near the blade. She lightly rubbed her thumb across the stone wondering why there wasn't one on the other side. She pushed a little harder, gasping in surprise when the blade extended, doubling in size.

"What happened?" Aren asked.

"Wow! Cool! I just pushed on this emerald, and the blade shot out!"

"Dang! It's a good thing you weren't pointing it at anything. That could have been bad," he said, noticing its lethal length. "Just be careful with that thing. You wouldn't want to have it pointing the wrong way if you accidentally push on that stone."

"Ya think?" she said. She pushed at the emerald again and the blade retracted. She was relieved to discover it required a bit more pressure than gently rubbing against it to get it to work. After pushing on it several more times, watching the blade shoot out and then retract, she decided to put it to rest for the night.

Aren was sitting on the branch with his legs dangling over the side, staring off into the distance.

Alexa asked, "Are you okay?"

"Just thinking," he said, as he bowed his head.

"That's becoming a habit of yours," Alexa teased.

He just snorted.

"Hey, what's up? What are you thinking about? Is it Nana?" she asked.

He felt guilty that his thoughts weren't about Nana. "No. Actually I was thinking about Emma."

"Oh. What about her?"

"I feel like a schmuck," he paused. When he didn't get a response from Alexa, he continued, "I invited her to the dance, and now I won't be there to take her."

"I'm sure she'll understand," Alexa said.

"How? How could she possibly understand? I won't be able to tell her that I can't take her! She won't know what happened to me. No one does! But that's not the worst part!" he said.

Alexa sat in silence waiting for him to continue.

"I was going to ask her to be my girlfriend, but ..."

"But what?"

He paused for a minute, then said in a small voice, "I chickened out."

"Oh," was all Alexa could think to say.

"You don't understand," he continued, "her dad is very strict. If I ask her to be my girlfriend, we'd have to keep our relationship a secret from him. He never lets her go anywhere or do anything. She can't even have friends over to her house, or hang out with her friends after school. Normally, she is allowed to go only to the library. So, if he agreed to let her go to the dance with me, and then I don't show up, he'll be furious and will probably take it out on her. She'll never be allowed to do anything ever again, thanks to me. I feel so bad. I really like her."

So that was why he had been spending so much time at the library, she thought. "I'm sorry Aren. I don't know what to say. Maybe we will be able to go back in time for the dance."

"I seriously doubt it."

With that they both laid out on their branches looking above at the specks of the night sky that peeked through the trees. The warmth of the still, fresh air was comforting. Before she knew it, sleep overtook Alexa as Bandit lay on her chest purring softly.

Aren removed the sword from its sheath. It shined brightly in the darkening night causing him to squint. As he stared at the blue crystal imbedded in the pummel, waves of water, like an ocean's torrent, appeared to churn within the stone. Aren rubbed at his tired eyes, sure that he was imagining things. When he looked again, the crystal was blue and still. His eyes wandered to the blade that was etched with intricate lines of beautiful swirls. The design doubled as his vision blurred from fatigue. Too tired to focus, he put the sword away. Using the satchel as a pillow, he turned on his side, adjusting the sword so he could pull it out swiftly if needed. Listening to his sister's sleep induced steady breathing brought on a hypnotic effect that caused Aren's eyelids to become heavy. With his hand on the hilt of the sword, Aren's mind and body finally gave in to the exhaustion that consumed him from the day's events and he drifted off into a sound sleep.

Chapter Eight

Alexa woke to the feeling of tiny feet walking across her neck. Bandit's fur tickled as it brushed lightly across her skin. She smiled, happy to see that he was still there and hadn't scurried off during the night. "Good morning little guy. Did you sleep well?" she whispered.

Bandit chirped, then rubbed up against her fingers. He began to purr as Alexa petted him.

"Don't get too used to this," she said. "I wouldn't want you to become too spoiled."

Aren stirred, scratching his outstretched hand along the tree branch. He bolted upright, gasping. His eyes were wild.

"Hey, Aren, what's wrong?" Alexa asked.

"Oh man. I woke up not knowing where I was. I hate it when that happens." He willed his pounding heart to calm down. He rubbed his hands over his face in an effort to wipe away the sleepy disorientation he felt. "Good morning, by the way. Did you sleep well?"

"Like a baby."

"Good. How's Bandit this morning?"

"Cute as ever," Alexa said, smiling. An involuntary groan escaped her as she sat up against the protest of her aching muscles.

"You okay Lex?" asked Aren.

"Oh my gosh. I feel as if I got hit by a train!" She plopped back down. "Every muscle in my body is screaming at me."

"Yikes! Must have been from the numerous beatings you took yesterday." Aren's mouth contorted in a sheepish grin.

"Dang! I didn't feel this sore yesterday."

"Well, if it makes you feel any better, I feel great!" he boasted.

"Ha ha. Don't make me sic Bandit on you! I'm sure he could do some pretty serious damage if he tried," she joked. She was happy to see that Aren appeared to be in a better mood this morning.

Aren laughed. "Your chin doesn't look too bad today."

"Well, gee, that's good!" She had forgotten about the scrape on her chin. It seemed to be the only part of her that didn't hurt.

"Do you need help getting up?" he offered.

Without answering him, she grimaced through the pain as she turned to her side and slowly pushed herself up into a sitting position. She dangled her legs over the branch, straightening them, while flexing her feet back and forth, stretching her muscles. Breathing in deep, she reached up with her arms as high as she could, feeling the burn in her abdomen. Slowly, she released and exhaled. Closing her eyes, she repeated the process, then concluded with a couple of controlled, deep breaths. *Ah, better*.

When she finished with her stretching performance, she opened her eyes to find Aren watching her with one elbow resting on his knee, and his chin resting in his hand. Bandit was perched on his other knee, also watching her with unblinking eyes.

Alexa looked from one to the other. "What's for breakfast?" she asked.

"Good question," Aren said. He reached into the satchel for the tube of wafers. Bandit scurried over and peered inside. "There is nothing for you in there, you little fur-ball, so back off." Aren shooed Bandit away.

Alexa took Bandit in her hands, and then placed him on her lap. When Aren handed her a wafer, Bandit stood on his tip-toes, reaching up to her fingers to inspect it. "You want to see this? I'm not sure it's something you would like to eat." She held the wafer in front of him. To her surprise, a tiny red tongue parted the fur below his eyes and licked at the wafer. As his tongue lapped several more times, Alexa spotted a little pink nose hidden in the fur above his mouth. "Oh my gosh, that is totally cute. Did you see his tongue and nose? I didn't even know he had a mouth."

"Of course he has a mouth. How do you think he eats? But you're right, that was pretty cute."

Alexa broke off a speck of the wafer and placed it in front of Bandit. His tongue jutted out and wrapped around the bit of food. Then the wafer disappeared into his fur. Within seconds, he puffed up into a ball, then let out what sounded like a burp. Both Alexa and Aren giggled at the sound of the tiny explosion.

"I think he liked it," observed Aren.

"I think so," Alexa giggled. She finished the rest of the wafer. "Yum," she said, as she tasted the flavors of blueberry pancakes with maple syrup, Canadian bacon, and poached eggs.

"That has always been one of my favorite breakfasts," said Aren. He placed the tube back in the satchel and retrieved the book.

Alexa moved over and sat next to Aren. Her eyes followed along as he read:

If you are reading this journal out loud, it might be wise from here on out to read silently. You never know who may be listening, the trees could have ears.

At those words, Aren and Alexa glanced at each other, then looked around. They didn't see anyone, and it didn't appear that the trees were listening. Even so, they decided it was probably a good idea to do as Nana instructed.

You are probably wondering why you were brought back so far away from Rheyaros. If you are reading this journal, that means we had been found, therefore our plans altered. Our ideal plan was to return you to Rheyaros at the rise of the Skylar Moon, and not a moment before.

"Skylar Moon?" Aren asked.

"Yes, remember the moon that appears once every thirteen years. The one that Nana talked about appearing on our fifteenth birthday this year," she reminded him.

"Oh, yeah. Now I remember."

"It's called the Skylar Moon because it protects the land. It's the only time the moon is blue."

“That’s right!” Aren admitted to himself that he didn’t retain as much information as Alexa did. She was like a sponge, her brain soaked up everything.

They kept reading: *It would have been too much of a risk to our people had you been released any closer. If the Xendors thought you were in Rheyaros, they surely would attack. With the Xendors on the hunt for the sword, they will stop at nothing to retrieve it. Remember that! Once the witch Mara discovers you have returned to Vesterra, she will be scouring the region with Xendors in search of you two. For this reason, it most certainly will not be safe to travel on the main path that leads directly to Rheyaros. Once they figure out you are not in Rheyaros, the Xendors will be searching not only for you, but your parents as well, assuming they are going to meet up with you. Of course, we know what happens when you ASS-U-ME! Therefore, for everyone's safety, no one, not even your parents, are aware of the location to which you have returned.*

There are many dangers in Vesterra. Stay alert and always beware of the enemy, for it lurks in the forest in many forms. The witch Mara has watchers in the forest so be very careful with whom you make contact.

"I'm not sure if I like the sound of that one," said Alexa.

"Sounds rather ominous, doesn't it?"

She nodded in agreement.

"We'll just have to be extra careful," he said.

"I wonder if Mom and Dad will be searching for us, or if they even know we are in Vesterra," Alexa said. "I can't wait to see them. It's been nearly three months since we saw them last."

"I don't know how they would know. But, I can't wait to see them either," Aren said. "This is some serious business we're caught up in. We need to be very careful and watchful as we go."

"Agreed," said Alexa.

Another reason for bringing you back so far away from Rheyaros is that there is also the danger of someone from the Other World accidentally slipping into our realm. It's happened before, and the outcome was not so pleasant. With them being far away from any one village, once found, it would be easier to send them back, ignorant of knowing where they truly were. We do not want to make a habit of having visitors from another realm drop in on us, or any other village, for that matter.

Aren wondered how often that happened. "We should go now. We'll read more later," he said. "It's already mid-morning and we've got a long way to go."

Alexa nodded in agreement, then scooped up Bandit and put him in her pocket. She grabbed hold of a branch and swung her body over, landing lightly on the ground.

Aren grimaced as he watched his sister's graceful decent. *Show off*, he thought.

Looking up, Alexa smirked when she noticed Aren was trying to figure out how he was going to get down without hurting himself.

He move to a narrower branch, wrapped his legs around it, then hugged the branch and turned upside down. Unlatching his legs, he dangled from the branch until he stopped swaying. Then he dropped, landing clumsily on his hands and knees. He stood up, adjusted the sword and the satchel, then raised his arms in the air, and announced, "The great Aren Rainz dismounts successfully! Now, let us go forth!"

Alexa just smiled and followed along. Bandit crawled out of her pocket and perched himself on her shoulder.

"Try not to boot any more rocks, okay," Aren teased, before stepping onto the trail.

"Whatever!"

They glanced in both directions to make sure no one was near, then started walking along the path towards Rheyaros.

The scenery was a multitude of splendor with the rocky hillside to their left, and the woods to their right. The grove of trees soon gave way to an array of flourishing vegetation that nestled on the bank of a slow flowing river. Near the water they spotted an animal trail between the plants that they decided would be a safer route rather than the openness of the main trail. Although the main trail was only a few yards away, there were more places to duck for cover along the animal trail.

"It's really pretty around here," observed Alexa.

"It is very deceiving. Beautiful, but extremely dangerous. For us anyway. We can't let the beauty of the place allow us to let down our guard."

They walked on in silence, scanning the trees and crevices between the rocks and boulders. The trail narrowed where it met the river, as signs of erosion were evident from the slow moving water that lapped across the sloping edges.

Alexa gave pause as Bandit bounced on her shoulder. He scurried down her body, then leapt off the toe of her shoe and scuttled to the edge of the river bank.

"Bandit! Stop!" Alexa screamed, afraid he was going to pitch into the river. She had no idea if he could swim.

He stopped short of the water in front of a small

patch of grass that had three yellow flowers blossoming between the thin blades. One of the flowers disappeared in his fur, then the stalk pulled out clean. After all three flowers had been consumed, Bandit turned to Alexa and jumped up and down.

"Well, I think we found what he likes to eat," proclaimed Alexa. She bent down to scoop up Bandit. Goosebumps immediately covered her body as her ears started to burn. She froze in place staring at the river. A splash of water slapped her hard in the face. She screamed, nearly dropping Bandit.

"Alexa! Get back!" Aren yelled, as he reached forward and yanked her away from the river. A slithering black hump crested the water, then sank below the surface. Before he could pull his sword, the creature was gone.

"What was that?" Alexa squeaked. She held Bandit close to her chest. He was wet, and trembling.

"It looked like some sort of huge water serpent! Look at the water. It looks like an oil spill where the thing touched the surface."

The tingling in her ears subsided as they watched the pewter ripples slowly dissipate, and the water return to its pristine blue hue.

"My ears started to burn, but there was no warning. Everything happened all of a sudden."

"Hmm, that's weird. Maybe we surprised it and woke

it up. Whatever it is, your ears confirmed that it's dangerous."

"Let's get out of here," pleaded Alexa.

"Gladly. Come on." Putting an arm around her shoulder, Aren guided her away from the river.

With Alexa taking the lead, they continued along the trail that deviated through a crevice between two huge boulders. The chasm was just wide enough for them to shuffle through without getting stuck. Alexa welcomed the confinement of her surroundings. The farther away she was from the river, the better, as far as she was concerned. To her dismay, the shelter was short lived and soon they were on the trail cresting the water's edge once again. With every sound of a wave lapping against the shoreline, Alexa would whip her head in the direction of the noise, ready to pull out the dagger. Because the ground was uneven, it was impossible for her to keep her eyes fixated on the river. She had to be careful where she was stepping for fear of tripping over a rock and falling in the water. The thought of encountering the serpent in its natural domain sent chills down her spine. It could see and breathe under water, and she could not.

Aren walked closely behind Alexa, with his hand on the hilt of his sword. He knew she was spooked, and did not blame her because her fears were valid. He was a bit shaken himself. The fact that her ears burned was proof that the creature would inflict harm on them. Next time he would be ready to defend her.

Chapter Nine

Standing by the door of the school library, Emma eyed the group sitting together in the middle of the quad. All four of them were friends with Aren and his sister. She debated on whether to approach them, or do her normal thing and go into the library. There were two boys, Dain and Josh, and two girls, Allison and Tara. She knew all of them as each were in at least one of her classes. They were a nice group of kids, but the only one she had ever really talked to before, and considered a friend, was Allison. Allison had such an approachable and bubbly personality, it was hard not to like her.

Even though it was a relatively small school where everyone pretty much knew everyone, Emma still didn't have many friends. She wasn't allowed to invite anyone to her house, nor was she allowed to go to anyone's house. The only place, besides school, that her father let her go to was the library. Her home life embarrassed her so much that she kept to herself. It always made her feel sad and left out when she would hear the other kids talk about how much fun they had over their weekends going to the movies, football games, dances or parties. She had been invited to go a few times, but her dad would never allow it. If she dared ask, he would scream at her and say the same thing every time: "*You are not going to grow up to be a loser and a tramp like your mother! You will make something of yourself young lady! How do you expect to be a smart and decent woman if you're out cavorting around like your mother always did!*" She hated that he always called her mother a tramp. Her mother wasn't anything like that. There were some things about her mom that her dad didn't know. Secrets that had been between her and Emma.

Standing there staring blindly at the group, she thought about when she had asked her dad for permission to go to the dance with Aren. She had been so nervous to the point of nearly throwing up as she approached him, knowing he would yell at her and say 'no', and then give her the speech he always gave her about her mother. But, she had to try anyway. Over and over, a hundred times, she had rehearsed in her mind how she would ask. But when the time finally came, as she looked at his abrasive face that was transparent with hatred, she had forgotten every word of what she intended to say. Instead, she nervously blurted out, "Dad! I'm 15. There is a dance. Aren Rainz asked me to go. Please Dad, can I? Just this once."

She hung her head down knowing she had blown it. That so wasn't what she wanted to say, or how she wanted to say it, but she guessed it was the gist of it. With tears threatening to spill from her eyes, she stared down at her feet as she stood there in front of him for what seemed an eternity, waiting for his rage. Standing in such close proximity of her father always made her anxious. She wished he would say something, anything, and hurry up about it, and get it over with. When finally he sighed heavily, she looked up into his angry eyes expecting the worst. Then, to her astonishment, he said 'fine'! She was so shocked, she stood frozen, not quite knowing what to say or do. He had never said 'yes' before. Well, he didn't actually say 'yes', he said 'fine', which meant 'yes', didn't it? When reality sunk in, she squealed, and then did something she hadn't done in years, she hugged her dad around his brawny shoulders.

He did not hug her back. Instead, he had taken her arms from around him, then held her at arms' length with his massive hands, more firmly than was necessary, as he stared into her tear filled eyes. Then, he laid out the conditions. Of course there would be conditions. He would drive her to the school. He would pick her up at ten o'clock sharp, no exceptions. If she couldn't follow those simple rules, she was grounded until she graduated from high school.

Nodding her head eagerly, failing at trying not to appear too excited, she agreed, "Of course! Of course!" Even though the dance didn't end until midnight, she didn't dare push it and ask for more time. Three hours at the dance with Aren Rainz was more than she had ever dreamed of! It would be the best three hours of her miserable life!

"If you dare try to dress or act like a tramp, like your mother, the consequences will be more severe!" he added. "Do you understand young lady?"

"Yes. Yes, I understand," she had said, eager to appease him. When in fact, she really didn't understand at all, because she didn't know what a tramp dressed like or acted like. Her mother had always dressed normal, like all the other mothers. She was also a loving, and hard working person, like most normal people. But, to satisfy him, she would agree.

The fact that Aren even invited her to the dance was amazing in itself, she thought. She wasn't sure what he saw in her when there were so many other girls to choose from. She was shy, but not awkward. She wasn't allowed to wear make-up, and she didn't wear expensive or trendy clothes. Her dad would never allow her to waste their money on that rubbish, as he called it. But, she was still cute enough, she guessed, in a plain sort of way. Then she thought that maybe it was her long blonde hair. Her hair was very pretty, after all. Or maybe it was her blue eyes? He had blue eyes, too! Her figure was average for a girl her age, and she was of average height. She came to the conclusion that she was just plain average, nothing more, nothing less. Aren seemed to like her more for who she was and not the material things that some people found important. That was what made him so awesome in her mind. He was so cute, nice, and genuine. Most cute guys were so full of themselves, but not Aren.

Emma didn't realize she was daydreaming until she heard someone calling out her name.

"Hey, Emma! Emma!" a girl's voice shouted.

Emma's eye came back into focus as she noticed Allison waiving her arms, trying to get her attention. All eyes at the table were on Emma. She waved back and decided to go join them. After all, she did want to ask them a question. Walking towards them, she noticed that not only was Aren absent from the group, but so was Alexa.

"Hi," she said, shyly.

They all greeted her in unison, while scooting over to make room for her.

"Hey, have a seat," Allison offered, patting the bench next to her. Her huge smile and cheeriness was always so inviting.

Emma sat, hugging her books. She felt embarrassed when Allison asked in a teasing manner, "You seemed really out of it over there, staring off into the oblivion. I called your name a dozen times. Are you okay?"

Blushing slightly, Emma said, "I, uh ... yes. I was just thinking about something."

"Yeah, what? Is he cute?" Allison joked, lifting her eyebrows up and down, causing her glasses to move slightly on the bridge of her nose.

The group all giggled and looked at Emma expectantly.

Emma fidgeted. Her mouth curled into a revealing smile. "He is, actually." She couldn't believe she just said that! And then she giggled.

"Oh, do tell, do tell!" Allison encouraged.

Both Allison and Tara leaned forward eager to hear about the cute boy, while Dain and Josh looked at each other wondering who it could be. All eyes were once again on Emma.

"Actually, I was wondering, um, if any of you knew where, uh, Aren is today? He usually meets me in the library, but, uh, I haven't seen him today," Emma said.

They all looked at each other, but none of them had seen him.

"Alexa isn't here either," Dain added, as he ran his fingers through his tussled hair. Emma wondered if Dain ever used a comb. His dark brown hair sat like a thick tangled mop on top of his head, but somehow, he wore it well.

"You're right. I haven't seen either one of them, and both of the them are in my first class," Tara said, cocking her head to the side, revealing the pink layer of hair that laid nearly concealed under her outer blonde layer. No one really knew what color Tara's hair was naturally because she dyed it so often. As colorful as her hair was, so were her clothes and jewelry. She didn't come across as a show off, she just liked to have fun with her appearance.

"Maybe they're sick," Allison said.

"Pfftthh," Josh's full lips fluttered. "The A-twins have never been sick a day in their lives," he said, using the nickname they had for Aren and Alexa. "Just like Mr. Ravend, here," he gestured towards Dain, who rolled his eyes. "Seriously, the A-twins are the only two kids I know that have never missed a day of school. And, I've known them since kindergarten."

"Well, there is a first time for everything, you know," Allison remarked, as she pushed her glasses up her slender nose.

"Well, if anyone cares, I won't be here for the rest of the week, starting tomorrow after school," Dain said to everyone. Or was he talking to everyone? He was looking at Emma as he spoke.

"I thought you were going to the dance?" said Allison.

"Oh, I'll be back in time for that," he said, not taking his eyes off Emma.

Is it my imagination, or is Dain staring at me? Emma thought.

"A three day weekend wasn't long enough for you, huh? Must be nice to go to school only two days this week!" Josh teased. "Where you goin' anyway?"

At that, Dain turned towards Josh and said, "Oh, it's

just some Ravend family thing out of town."

"Cool! Can I come too?" Josh pleaded. "I would love to miss out on that science test we have on Friday."

"Uh, no. Sorry buddy. Family only, otherwise you know I would let you tag along." He gave Josh a playful punch on the arm as he said it, then turned his attention back to Emma.

Emma diverted her eyes feeling a little uncomfortable. No one else in the group seemed to notice Dain looking at her. She suddenly felt mortified thinking there might be a booger in her nose. Slowly bringing her hand up, she gave her nose a sly swipe. She felt silly, but was relieved to find nothing there.

Just then, the bell rang to announce that lunch was over. They all stood and started heading towards their classes.

Before they parted ways, Dain asked Emma, "So, Emma, are you going to the dance also on Saturday?"

"Yes, I'll be going for a short while. I have to leave at ten though," she said.

"Awesome! I'll see you there!" he said, then bounded off towards his class with Josh, as the girls all headed in the opposite direction.

"Wow," Dain whispered to Josh when they were far enough away that none of the girls could hear him, "I never noticed how cute Emma was before."

"Dude! Seriously? I think you might have some competition there. Didn't you hear her say that Aren usually meets her in the library? Sounds as if he might already have his sights on her," said Josh.

Dain considered what Josh said. He casually glanced back and saw the girls as they were turning the corner, near their classroom. Changing the subject he said, "Speaking of sights, I bet I can get a bull's-eye at thirty yards in Archery today!"

"You get a bull's-eye every day. You and the A-twins are like the supreme masters at archery, so, no bet. How bout we bet on something else."

"Yeah, like what?"

"Like, um, who gets a better score on our math test today!"

"Right, like that's a fair bet. You are the math geek of the universe."

Laughing, they shoved each other, then headed to their Archery class.

Chapter Ten

Following the curvature of the mountain, water poured out from deep within the recesses, forming a sheer, velvety sheet that plummeted into a wide pool at the base of the mountain. The constant push of water spilled over the rim of the pool, spreading like soft veils across the rocky slabs. The current passed through and around the roots that grew in its path from the massive tree. Past the tree, the river parted, flowing in opposite directions, uniting with the other waterways of Vesterra.

The relaxing sound of the steady stream did nothing to sooth Yasmin. She sat in the chair staring out into the landscape wondering how it was possible that a place so incredibly beautiful could be so dangerous.

As she watched Erik walk in, all she could think to say was, "Well?"

"I'm sorry, Nana Gazelle is dead," Erik said.

"I know. I felt it when she died." Yasmin’s heart ached. "But, what about the children?"

Erik shook his head. "I don't know."

"What do you mean you don't know?" Grief and fear threatened to overtake her.

Erik sat in front of his wife, clasping her hands,

rubbing them tenderly as he spoke, "When I arrived at the cabin, the inside was destroyed. Someone had ransacked the place. The chest was empty, the sword gone." He paused, taking a deep breath. "There were no signs of the children anywhere. But, it seems they most likely escaped through a tunnel."

"A tunnel? What tunnel?" she asked.

"There was a tunnel, rather, what appeared to be a tunnel, from behind the stairwell. But it was caved in, filled with rocks and boulders. There was dust everywhere. I could not tell where the tunnel led, but I'm sure the kids escaped."

"How can you be so sure?" her voice was strained. "If they escaped, then they must be in Vesterra somewhere. That is where Nana would have instructed them to go, knowing the Skylar Moon was near. We need to send seekers out to find them!"

"My love," he said, softly, "I trust that Nana did what she was tasked to do and taught the children well. We will find them."

A knock at the parlor door interrupted them. A tall slender elf dressed in protective leather gear, barged in.

"Lady Yasmin. Sir Erik." He gave a quick nod, then continued, "Forgive me for intruding. There is news from a watcher. Odin was spotted in Vesterra. He rides with two men. He is seeking information on a boy and a girl!" he blurted.

Yasmin stood, pulling her hand from Erik's. "When? Where? How do you know?"

"Near first early light. He was inquiring with the Gnomes of Girk near Dragon Fire," he said.

"And what did the gnomes tell him?" she asked.

"No one had seen them."

"I don't trust the gnomes! They would sell their own young if offered enough gold," she said, with disgust.

"My lady Yasmin, it is true that greed invades the souls of many, but not all. There are some very honorable gnomes," he said. "The Gnomes of Girk are my friends, and have served me well."

"As you say." She was not convinced.

"Harbin, send out your most trusted seekers," Erik commanded. "Two parties, one to the north, the other south. Tell them they are searching for Aren and Alexa. They are fifteen years of age. Black hair, and blue eyes. They will probably be dressed a little, uh, strangely. Return immediately with any word on their whereabouts as soon as it is known. Remind the seekers, this is not to be discussed with anyone. They are to provide protection to the children and return them safely. Mara's men must not find them!"

"Yes, Sir Erik," Harbin said.

"Remember, it will be incredibly dangerous for our people if Mara learns that the children returned here before the night of the Skylar Moon. If the children are found, keep them hidden and off of the main trails if at all possible. Also, I think it would be best if our people did not know they were in Vesterra. Only the seekers and we should know. We need everyone to go about their business as usual so the Xendors will not be suspicious of us. If they think Aren and Alexa are in Rheyaros, who knows what they will do. I don't want to put our people in any more danger than they already are."

"I understand. I will send the seekers out immediately. We will find your children."

"One more thing," said Erik, "with what men you have left, I want you to place them at the top of the falls and around the perimeter until further advised."

"I will get on it immediately." He bowed slightly, then left the room.

As he left, Yasmin walked out on the balcony and looked about her surroundings. Searching for any deficiency, she took in all the different spots she knew guards would be placed. There would be two men covering each other in several covert locations throughout Rheyaros. With the coverage, she knew there was a very slim chance of anyone bypassing the river, or the great tree, penetrating their haven without being seen. But the experienced were few. Too many elves had been lost in the attack thirteen years ago, and still, there weren't enough of age to be trained properly.

"I cannot stand to sit here while my children are out there somewhere. They do not know this place."

"Yasmin, they will be fine. They are both very smart, very capable children. They are more familiar with this place than you, or they, probably realize."

"They haven't been in Vesterra since they were two! They've never been to Rheyaros! They know nothing of this place except what they have learned through Nana's story telling!" Yasmin shouted.

He appeared behind her on the balcony, and wrapped his arms around her in a loving embrace. As she laid her head against his chest, he said, "Would it make you feel better if I went with the seekers?"

"No," she said. "It would make me feel better if *we* went with the seekers."

"But, it will be too dangerous."

"You know I can handle my own. I'm no slouch."

He kissed the top of her head. "You are the most incredible woman I know. So fierce, yet so gentle. However, one of us should stay here, in case they show in Rheyaros."

She thought on it for a few moments. Turning to face him, she said, "I will give the seekers until tomorrow. If they do not find our children, then we can ride out together."

"We will give them until the noon hour, then we will ride." He kissed her gently on the lips, and hugged her tightly. "You are my life, Yasmin. I love you more than anyone should be allowed to love another. I would not be able to forgive myself if anything happened to you."

"Well then, I suppose we shouldn't let anything happen to me, now shall we," she teased.

Staring at the massive tree branches jutting out before him brought his thoughts back to the cabin. "The cabin was in shambles. I repaired what I could. I also contacted the school to let them know there was a family emergency and the kids would be away for a while. Hopefully, no one will go to the cabin looking for them."

Yasmin tensed in his arms. Turning her back against his chest, she focused her eyes on the landscape, lost in thought. She silently vowed to kill the witch Mara and her barbarian warrior if anything happened to her children. She would not let them hurt her family ever again, or destroy her people. *I will hunt her down and kill her!*

Chapter Eleven

A soft trickling sound crept through the air as the river left behind the serene beauty of the forest and entered a rocky gorge. At the edge of the forest the water pooled, then spilled in sheets over a stony ridge onto a wide bed of rocks. Moving swiftly, the flow soon became a roar as the riverbed narrowed, forcing the water to push its way wildly over moss covered boulders. Large waves tossed violently, creating powerful rapids as the river raced through the narrowing passage.

Surveying the area, they knew following the river was no longer an option. The route was too perilous and impassable. Their only choice was the main path that meandered through the canyon.

The heat from the sun was diminished by the cool breeze that wafted from the rapids. Aren decided to sit under a tree away from the misty dampness of the river so that he could look at the map.

Alexa sat next to him, keeping a watchful eye on Bandit, who had jumped from her shoulder onto the ground. He appeared to be sniffing the air, then slowly started wandering toward another tree where a treasure of tiny flowers awaited him at the base. He inched along, taking a few small steps, as if he was stalking his prey, ready to pounce. “He is so stinkin' cute,” Alexa whispered to herself.

Aren was studying the map with intense interest. "These letters and symbols are so small, they are hard to decipher. I wish I had a magnifying glass or something to see them better." He spread his thumb and forefinger over the area of the map he wanted to be bigger as he would have done on his computer screen. To his astonishment, the map leapt from the page in magnified form. "Oh my gosh! Did you see that Lex? Look! The map! It grew!"

"Whoa! How did you do that?"

"I don't know. I was just thinking how it would be cool if I could make the image larger with my fingers like I do on my computer tablet, and then when I tried it, bam! Just like that, it worked!" Aren’s excitement grew as he perused the map.

Alexa’s eyebrows rose at the sight. "Awesome! That sure does make it easier to read."

After finding their location, Aren’s eyes scanned across the map to the area of Rheyaros where he noticed what looked like a statue of a man pointing to the north. It was situated in front of the huge tree, near the river. He wondered at the statue's significance, but was more intrigued that there was a landmark that would be easy to spot. His eyes moved back to their current location. "According to this map, it looks as if we're going to have to walk through the canyon, directly on the path. There really isn't any way around it."

"Okay. I wonder if there will be places to hide, just in case?" Alexa peered at the map.

"I'm not sure what this is, but it says 'Krug's Cave'." Aren pointed at a spot on the map near the edge of the canyon.

"Krug? Isn't that the troll?"

"The troll? Ugh. Not sure we want to be meeting up with a troll!"

"Is there any other way around the cave?" Alexa sounded concerned.

"Doesn't look like it. Behind the cave is a stream that eventually runs in the same direction as the main trail. In order to get to the stream, we have to walk right by the opening to the cave. We might be able to climb over some rocks and bypass its entrance. I guess we won't know until we get there."

"Oh great, just great!" She threw her hands in the air.

"Maybe the troll doesn't live there anymore. Or, maybe, he'll be sleeping. Maybe he sleeps during the day. Let's not panic just yet," said Aren.

"Okay, okay. I'm sure he's a nice troll. Hopefully, he doesn't eat people."

"Don't worry, you're too skinny anyway. He would probably prefer something with a little more meat on its bones, like me!" Aren said, flexing his muscles trying to lighten the moment. "But, I'm not scared. I'll just pull out the sword and cut him in two! Whack, whack!" he said, as he slashed his arm through the air as he would the sword. "Just like that!"

"Uh, huh," Alexa said, doubtful.

"In any event, I don't think we'll be wanting to be his guest for dinner, if you know what I mean."

"I know exactly what you mean. I will politely decline his invitation."

Aren's demeanor turned serious. "Hopefully, it won't come to that." He turned the pages of the book to where they had last left off and they both started reading.

Aren, it is imperative for the survival of our people, and those living in the region, that you arrive in Rheyaros on or before the night of the Skylar Moon with the sword. The sword must never find its way in the hands of the enemy. Keep it with you at all times!

"Okay, but why me? Why do I have to be the one to return the sword and not you, or someone else?"

Alexa shrugged her shoulders. "Heck if I know."

You and the sword are the key. Remember this: "By rights, the tail of Jericho brightens the night by the light of the moon". Study the map closely.

He turned the page, but there was no more writing. "That's it? What does that mean? What is the tail of

Jericho?"

"Jericho was the king of the Mer-folk," said Alexa. "He died when his trident penetrated his tail, impaling him to the ocean floor, killing him but saving the Mer-folk from the sea demons."

"I remember the story, but what does all that have to do with me? Specifically Jericho." He stuffed the book back in the satchel feeling frustrated at his lack of understanding.

"I'm not sure, but we'll figure it out eventually, maybe." Her voice trailed off, short on confidence.

After getting his fill, Bandit scurried back to Alexa when he saw her stand. She picked him up and placed him on her shoulder.

"Aren!" Alexa's voice was strained.

"What?"

"My ears are starting to tingle. Are they red?" She pushed her hair behind her ears exposing them.

At the sight of the vivid redness, Aren jumped up and pulled out the sword. Alexa grabbed for the dagger. They spun around towards the river as a large wave billowed towards them. A scaly black hump broke the surface then sunk back into the water creating a torrent of grey swelling rolls. Aren and Alexa backed away from the river as a two-headed black serpent exploded out of the water, towering before them. The heads were weaving back and forth, hissing as slithering tongues flickered between huge fangs. Its mouths gnashed violently at the air. The serpent loomed above, staring at Aren and Alexa with its beady yellow eyes.

Aren stabbed the sword in warning in the direction of the serpent. The sunlight reflected off the blade in a blazing flash of light, momentarily blinding the two-headed beast. It recoiled, then plunged heavily into the water. Huge bubbles burst as it thrashed wildly. Then, as quickly as it appeared, the serpent disappeared leaving behind the oily, grey sheen.

"Holy cow!" Aren yelled. "What the heck was that?"

"That was the biggest dang snake I've ever seen! With two heads no less!" Alexa squeaked. She held tight to the dagger, pointing it towards the river. Her hands were shaking. "Look at my ears. I no longer feel them burning. Are they red?"

"No," Aren said. "It must have left." He stared out over the river trying to see where the serpent may have gone but saw no trace of it.

When she noticed Aren sheathing the sword, Alexa felt it must be safe to return the dagger as well. It was then that she realized Bandit was hiding inside her pocket, scared and trembling. She peered inside but decided not to take him out yet.

"Geezzz. I hate to admit it, but that was a bit scary. We should probably get moving. Thank goodness we'll be going away from the river," Aren said. "For a while anyway."

Looking behind her at the spot where the serpent had

made its appearance, Alexa felt relieved as they stepped onto the path that would lead them into the canyon. Although she knew there could be dangers on this path as well, she thought nothing could be as bad as a giant two-headed snake. Unless, of course, they ran into the Xendors.

They walked silently, navigating their way between the huge boulders that formed imposing walls of granite stonework. The sounds of their footsteps echoed as they trekked along the gravel covered ground. Waves of heat danced off the rocks as the sun beat straight down. The lack of a breeze made the air stifling. As the path climbed, the terrain became uneven with jagged rocks jutting out of the ground everywhere. Their pace slowed as the hike became laborious.

"Dang, it’s hot in this canyon." Alexa wiped the sweat from her forehead with the back of her hand.

"It sure is," agreed Aren.

"How much farther do you suppose we have to go?" Alexa asked, relieved that the path had finally evened out.

"Well, according to the map, see where the canyon slopes down," he said, pointing through a rocky archway, "just past the base, it curves around to the left a bit. Then, to the right is Krug's Cave. The path keeps going to the left, but we need to somehow go to the right, in front of the cave, to get to the stream."

"At least we'll be going downhill! This climb is a killer

in this heat."

"Do you want to take a break?" asked Aren.

"No, I'd rather get out of this canyon and back in the shade of the trees. There are trees down there, right?"

"I sure hope so."

Alexa peeked inside her pocket where Bandit had decided to stay. As she pulled it open, he looked up at her with his big blue eyes, then closed them. His little body seemed to be bobbing up and down with shallow breaths.

"How's Bandit?" Aren asked, when he noticed Alexa checking in on him.

"I think he is panting. It must be too hot for him out here," she said. "I hope he'll be okay."

"It shouldn't take us too long to get to the bottom, as long as we don't meet up with any obstacles, or do something stupid like hurting ourselves falling," he said.

They moved on, stepping carefully over and around the rocks that cluttered the pathway. Shadows slowly crawled up the canyon walls as the sun passed overhead, providing some shade as they walked. Alexa noticed the closer they got to the bottom, the less Bandit panted. She slowed briefly to peek inside her pocket again. He looked up at her, then shifted, but stayed where he was. He seemed to be doing better.

"Eww. What's that smell? Is it me?" Alexa asked, sniffing at her armpits. She smelled of sweat, but that wasn't the odor that was permeating the air.

"I don't think it's either one of us," Aren said, in a hushed tone. "My guess is we're pretty close to the troll's cave. It should be just around the corner here."

They crept along the boulders as quietly as possible. To the left, brush took over where the boulders had lined the pathway leading into a forest of trees. Aren snuck a peek around the rocks that were to the right. There he saw a wide pad of course sand that led the way to the entrance of a dark cave. Huge boulders framed the opening of the cave on both sides. In front of the entrance was an alcove where a large pot sat above a burning fire.

"What do you see?" whispered Alexa.

Aren stepped back. "I saw a cave, but no troll. I think what we smell is whatever it is cooking in the pot outside the cave," he whispered. "I don't know how we are going to get past if there is a troll in there."

"I want to see," Alexa whispered, pushing her way past Aren. She crouched down and peered around the boulder. Aren stepped behind her, and peeked out over her head. "I see our dilemma," she whispered.

"Maybe we can sneak over to those rocks on the other side of the path. From there we should be able to get a better view inside the cave. When we're sure the coast is clear, we can make a run for it and hide behind the bushes, then sneak our way to the stream. What do you think?"

"My ears aren't tingling, so I say we go for it."

Chapter Twelve

They crouched between the two boulders listening for any signs of the troll. After several minutes of sitting silently, Aren said, "I'm going to sneak a peek. Stay down." He poked his head above the rock then quickly ducked back down.

"Well?"

Aren shook his head. "Nothing."

Oh no! Alexa thought as she felt a slight tingle in her ears. She tapped Aren on the shoulder then pointed at her ears. Moving her hair aside to show him, the tips were starting to turn red, but not yet bright.

Aren snuck another quick peek over the rock, but still did not see the troll.

"Do you hear that?" Alexa whispered. She could feel Bandit shaking in her pocket.

Aren listened intently. He heard a faint rumbling sound. "I think it's coming from the forest," he whispered. He cocked his head to the side straining to hear. "Sounds like horses," he determined, as the sound grew louder. "More than one."

They both stood, exposing their backs to the opening of the cave as they stooped over the bigger of the two rocks to peer at the trail that led into the forest. The tingling grew fiercer in Alexa's ears. Just then, the two of them were yanked backwards, the back of their legs scraping across the rock. Giant hands covered their mouths. A tight grip pinned their arms to their sides. They both squirmed trying to free themselves as they were dragged into the darkness of the cave. The restraint around them eased, as they were spun around until they were face to face with the troll.

Aren pushed Alexa farther back into a crevice with one hand, as he reached for the sword with the other. "Get away from ..." he started to threaten.

"Shhhh." Spittle sprayed from the troll's mouth as he brought one of his massive fingers before it, motioning them to be quiet.

Aren pulled at the sword that glowed as it slid out of its scabbard. But, the troll was quick and placed his hand firmly over Aren's, forcing it back in its place. There had been just enough light that they both had caught a glimpse of the troll's face. His head was big, and weathered with deep creases. A brow ridge covered with unruly eyebrows hid his sunken eyes. His flat nose spread wide above his enormous moth.

"I think he's trying to help us," Alexa whispered.

"Find refugeth here," the troll said, with a thick tongue, in a low gravelly voice. "The Xendorths are coming." He reached towards Alexa and she flinched as he gently pulled her hair over her glowing ears. "Keep thoseth covered," he warned. With that, the troll turned and walked towards the exit of the cave, as the thunderous sound of hoofs grew louder.

From the darkness of their hiding spot, Aren and Alexa could see just how massive the troll was when he stepped out into the light. His head sat atop broad shoulders that sprouted large and hairy arms. Legs as thick as tree trunks supported his ample body. On bare feet that were crusted over with dirt, he lumbered, hunched over, to the cooking pot. Casually he stirred its contents with a large bone just as the Xendors closed in.

Focusing on Krug, Aren wondered how it was possible for a creature so huge to be able to sneak up on them without being heard.

A small cloud of dust formed as three mighty horses came to an abrupt halt on the sand, shy of the main trail. The horses snorted, stomping powerfully as their riders labored to still their movements. The beasts were enormous, shiny black, with long mains and tails. Their silver eyes were ghostly and frightful in contrast to their coat. The front of their hooves came to a point, like talons, biting into the ground. As intimidating as the horses were, so much more were their riders. Odin, and two other Xendors, sat tall upon the impressive beasts. Their looks boasted of arrogant superiority as they took up their positions in a line before Krug. Odin, clearly the leader, sat center, with the two other

Xendors posted on either side of him.

The troll turned his head up and snarled at the sight of the Xendors who were invading his turf.

"Well, good day to you, too, Krug," Odin bellowed, as if greeting a friend.

"Whath do you wanth?" Krug growled.

"We were just passing by and thought we would check in on you. You must get lonely out here all by yourself." As if trained to do so, his two sentries chuckled in unison.

Krug noticed each of Odin's men carried a slender wicker cage attached to the side of their saddles. Between the bars, Krug could see the beady red eyes of ravens peering through. Their pointy black beaks poked through the narrow slats. The confines of the cages made it impossible for the birds to spread their wings or move about. Krug felt sorry for them and wished he could rescue them, but he knew it would be useless, for they were well trained, and would fly right back to the witch, Mara. Krug scowled and glared at Odin. His lips fluttered as a growl passed through his barred teeth.

"I can see you are happy to see us. Well, we'd love to stay for dinner, it smells so, uh, appetizing," Odin said, crinkling his nose. "Unfortunately, we've got more pressing matters at hand. Say, you wouldn't have happened to have seen a boy and a girl wandering these parts, would you?" Odin asked, raising an eyebrow.

"If I hath, they would be stewin' in my poth!" Krug

grumbled.

Odin howled a fake laugh, and on cue, his two sentries snickered also. "You are quite the host, Krug! I would expect nothing less of such a menacing troll as you." Then his look became serious as he turned on his mount and peered into the cave. His two men turned their heads following his gaze.

While their heads were turned Krug casually remove the bone from the pot and held it at his side, ready to strike.

Seeing nothing but blackness, Odin turned back to face Krug, noticing the way he was now holding the bone. He looked from the bone to Krug's face.

Krug slowly raised the bone and plopped it back into the pot, stirring one-handed while never taking his eyes off Odin.

Odin glared at him, then said in a threatening voice, "If you happen upon those two children, a boy and a girl, you will make sure to hold them for me, along with all their possessions. I will be back in a day or two. If I learn you have defied me, your fate will be the same as Kreega's! I swear it!" Before he could get a response from Krug, he turned his mount and rode off with the sentries following behind him.

Infuriated by the mention of Kreega, Krug launched the stirring bone at the Xendors hitting the last horse in line on the hind quarter as it was turning to enter the canyon. The horse bucked and spun nearly knocking its rider off. The

Xendor struggled to stay in his saddle, fighting to gain control of the wild beast. When he finally calmed his horse, he turned towards Krug and threatened, "You will pay for that troll!" Then he kicked his horse and rode off into the canyon.

Krug growled loudly at the Xendors as they rode off. “How dareth the name of my precious Kreega pass histh slimy lips!” he huffed, storming over to the stirring bone, picking it up. He swung the bone down hard on a rock. Bits and pieces of the rock flew everywhere. He wished the rock was Odin's head, and smashed it again. “We'll seeth who sufferths if they return!” he seethed. He looked at the bone in his hands noticing a new fracture that now blemished its features from the bashing it just took. Had the two children not been hunkered down in his cave, he would have cracked open the Xendors's heads instead of punishing the rock. Those were Yasmin's children in his cave, he knew. He owed it to her to help her kin, remembering how she had helped him once.

He ambled back to the pot, plunging the bone in, stirring vigorously, taking his frustrations out on the hot, bubbly brew. His lips fluttered as if he was grumbling to himself. Deep in thought, he had momentarily forgotten he was not alone until he felt a gentle hand touch his arm. His shoulders slumped as his head dipped precariously over the pot. Using the bone as leverage, he pushed back when a pungent plume of steam enveloped his face. Droplets streamed down his cheeks from the condensation, or were they tears?

Alexa noticed Krug's eyes were bloodshot when he turned his head towards her. He stepped away from her and sat down heavily on a flat rock near the entrance to the cave. Hunched over, he appeared to be inspecting the dirt on his hands that were resting on his knees. Alexa sat next to him thankful to not be standing right next to the offensive smelling brew that permeated the air. She wondered what it was that he was cooking in the pot causing it to smell so badly.

Aren leaned against the entrance to the cave as he closely watched his sister and Krug. Noticing Alexa's ears were no longer red, he figured Krug must not be a threat, it was the Xendors that had made her ears go crazy.

It wasn't until Alexa's ears stopped burning that they felt it was safe to leave the confines of the cave. They had watched from the darkness as the Xendors rode up and confronted Krug. They both had tensed when Odin had turned to look in the cave. Alexa had covered her ears with her hands fearing he might be able to see the red glow, even though her hair was covering them. Aren's hand had never left the hilt of the sword. He was ready this time! Aren prepared himself to charge when the Xendor, whose horse was hit by the bone, threatened Krug. They had both breathed a sigh of relief when the Xendor rode off, but then were startled to witness Krug's violent bone bashing behavior.

"Thank you for helping us," Alexa said, softly.

"You are Yasthmin's childrenth," he said.

"You know our mother?"

"Yeth. She helpeth me once." Krug looked sad.

"How?" Alexa asked. Bandit popped out of her pocket and nestled himself on her shoulder. She had almost forgotten he was there because he had grown so still. She reached up with a finger and tickled his fur as he rubbed up against her neck.

"A long time ago, there wath a war. The Xendorth came looking for you two. They dith not believe that we hath not seen you. They thought we, me and my Kreega, were hiding you. They were wild and mad. They stormeth inside my cave, and drug my Kreega outh by ropes around her legs. Mara, the witch was there. She useth her magic to throw me againsth the rocks righth there where she helth me with her power," he said, pointing with his huge finger to the large wall of boulders that blocked the view of the canyon. "I was uthless. I could noth help my Kreega. They slammed her againth the rocks over there," he pointed a few feet away from where he had been assaulted. "The rocks broke and crashth down on top of her. When the Xendorths left, I was helpless. I could barely move. Your mother and another olth lady hath come by and saw our peril. Your mother trieth to free my Kreega from the rocks that were piled on her. They trieth to save her, but it wath no uth. Then, your mother came to me. She hath tears running down her eyeths. She wath tending to my wounths, but just kept saying, 'I'm sowry'. Then, her and the olth lady helpth drag me next to Kreega, so I could holth her one last time before she dieth. Her body and headth were broken, and so wath my heart," he said, with tears flooding his eyes, and snot dribbling from his nose.

Not knowing what to say, Alexa bent her head down and rubbed her finger along Bandit's head. He had jumped to her lap and was looking up at Krug with sad eyes during the telling of his story. They all stayed silent, allowing Krug his moment of grief.

After several moments, Krug sucked in a deep breath, then wiped at the snot running from his nose with the back of his finger. He flung the wet goo to the ground, then wiped his hand on the backside of his pants.

Gross, thought Aren.

Krug's eyes melted when he looked down, noticing Bandit for the first time. "Aw, heth so cute," he said, as he reached over to tickle the top of Bandit's head with his finger. Alexa was thankful that it was not the same finger he had used to wipe his snot with. "Whath is his name?"

"It's Bandit."

"Bandith," he repeated, puckering his lips out as he made a cooing noise.

This made both Aren and Alexa smile. The last thing they expected from a troll was the display of such sweet and gentle behavior. They had always imagined trolls being mean and vicious, but Krug kept surprising them.

"I'm Alexa, and he is my brother, Aren."

"I Krug," he said, with a half crooked smile.

"Hey, Krug, what is it that you have stewing in that pot anyway?" Aren asked. "It really stinks!"

Krug let out a little chuckle, his shoulders shook up and down. "It's a loth of different things. If I find something dead or rotthen, I puth it in the pot."

"Uh, and you eat that stuff?" Aren asked, with disgust.

Krug chuckled again. "No. I'm a vegitharian," he said, smiling broadly. "I don't eat junk food." Then he laughed loud, throwing his head back. His smile spread the width of his face exposing a mouth full of wide flat teeth. His laugh was contagious, causing Aren and Alexa to join in. Even Bandit seemed to think it was funny for he was bobbing up and down on Alexa's lap.

"Do you think that's funny, or are you relieved that he is a vegetarian?" Alexa teased Bandit. That made Krug laugh even more.

When the laughing subsided, Aren asked, "So, if you

don't eat it, what do you do with it?"

"It smellth so bad, it keepth people away."

"But, don't you get lonely?" Alexa asked.

"Noth really," Krug said, "although, I mith my Kreega. Sometimeth your mother visith me. She alwayth bringsth a bunch of flowerth that she holdth close to her nose so she doesenth have to smell the stink."

"So, what do you do all day?" Alexa asked.

"I have a garden over there," he said, pointing around the side of the cave. "Come look."

They followed Krug around the back side of the cave, and through some shrubs that followed a stream bed. The water was crystal clear, deep and swift. Krug bent down to wash his hands, his eyes constantly searching the stream.

Alexa noticed how Krug kept his eyes on the water until he was done. She wondered if he was looking for the serpent.

The creature was quickly forgotten as they stepped through the bushes into Krug's garden. It was an impressive sight with organized rows of different fruits and vegetables. The garden was very well tended, neat and clean, free of weeds. There were several rows of eggplant, cauliflower, tomatoes, squash, pumpkins, carrots, and other vegetables that Aren and Alexa didn't recognize. Leafy greens and fragrant herbs separated the vegetables from the fruit trees. There were three trees each of lemons, oranges, apples, peaches, and a pungent red fruit with a prickly flower at the tip.

"Thith ith where I sthpend a lot of my time," Krug said. He walked over to the trees and picked up one of the red fruits that had dropped to the ground. "Thith fruit smellth really bad when it roths, but tasteth good when its fresth. Thith helpth give my pot a bad smell."

"Whoa," Aren said. "You do this all by yourself? I mean, you grow this garden, and weed it and everything?"

"Ah, huh," said Krug, with a proud nod of his head.

"Wow!" they both said at the same time. They were surprised and impressed that a troll, of all creatures, would have such a beautiful, well-kept garden. They watched as Krug walked around picking a few of the fruits and vegetables, gathering them in his massive arms. When he had an arm full, he nodded with a smile to have them follow him back to the cave. Alexa again noticed how Krug watched the stream out of the corners of his eyes as they passed by.

Chapter Thirteen

They followed Krug into the darkness of the cave, then lost sight of him momentarily as he turned sideways disappearing into the wall. They both stopped, wondering how he had done that. Then Krug poked his head back out from behind the wall and motioned for them to follow. He hadn't actually walked through the wall as it appeared. The colors all blended together so well in the darkness that there was the illusion it was one solid piece of rock.

Aren slid the sword partially out of its scabbard to give them enough light to follow Krug through the maze of twists and turns. He figured that either Krug could see in the dark, or he knew the way by heart.

Krug's underground living area was a large cavern illuminated by several torches. In one corner, there was a table and two seats made from large tree trunks. Near the table, water trickled continuously from a small fissure into a rock basin that Krug used as a washing bin for his food and utensils. On the other side of the room was a long slab of granite that was his bed. A pile of tattered blankets were crumpled up on one end.

"Krug, have you ever seen the two headed water serpent?" Alexa asked. They were in the well-hidden living quarters of his cave, preparing to eat a meal consisting of fruits and vegetables that Krug had made for them.

"Instherpia," Krug said in his thick tongue.

"Inserpia?" Alexa confirmed.

"Yeth! One day she will be sthewing in my pot!" Krug said.

Alexa noticed Krug's speech was getting better the more he talked, or she was getting used to his thick-tongued speech. "Is she really dangerous?" asked Alexa, not really wanting to hear the answer.

"Vvvery!" His lips furled as he said it.

"Before we entered the canyon, she popped out of the river and scared us half to death," Alexa said.

"Hmm," Krug stared down at his food. He looked over at Alexa, concern etched on his face as he thought about what she said. "Instherpia could eat you whole. I've stheen her snag a deer by the water. Both her headths fought for the prizth and ended up ripping the deer in half. She ith very vithous. She tried to get my Kreega once!" He let out a growl. "But, I scared her off with a sthick of fire!" He thrust his arm out holding an invisible torch, showing them how he fended off Inserpia. "I see her sthwim by every oneth in a while, but she never pokeths her head out of the water."

"Does she ever come onto land?" Alexa asked.

"Sometimeths," he said. "But, you need to sthay away from the river ath much ath you can so she doesthn't see you."

"How are we supposed to do that?" Aren asked. "Unless we walk on the main trail which, clearly is too dangerous. The Xendors are sure to find us then. The only other way I could see to go, according to the map, is by following the streams and the river."

"I know a way that will take you to Dragon Fire," Krug said. "I will sthow you in the morning. You can sthay here for the nighth where you will be sthafe."

Aren and Alexa looked at each other for confirmation. They both shrugged their shoulders, then Aren said, "Okay, since its already starting to get dark outside, we'll stay. Thank you."

Bandit seemed content as he nibbled on little pieces of food that Krug had prepared specifically for him. Alexa was amazed that Krug, with his massive hands, could cut such teeny bite size pieces that were just the right size for the little pinquist. Bandit seemed to enjoy his dinner as much as Aren and Alexa did. Krug had tossed together a tasty mix of fruits and vegetables that were ripe and full of flavor, adding a pinch of herbs to bring it all together. He had served the meal on big boat-shaped leaves. After they all had finished eating, Krug showed Aren and Alexa the rest of his living quarters.

"Here ith the bathing room," he said. The room was through a passageway behind the dining area. It was humid and very warm inside. Steam rose from a wide pool as water poured through a hole on one side, and filtered out another hole on the opposite side, creating a constant flow of fresh water.

Admiring the natural tub, Alexa thought how wonderful a hot bath would feel right now.

"Over there," Krug pointed behind another wall, "well, thaths the releasthing room." He seemed to blush as he said it.

"A releasing room? What's that?" asked Aren.

"Uh, you know," Krug stammered, "iths where you go, um, well, where you releasth."

Aren walked over and peeked around the corner. It was a latrine! And what a latrine it was! The toilet was a large obsidian rock shelf with a oval cutout that went as far back as the wall. A continuous stream of water spilled from the wall behind it, into the oval cutout. Fragrant ivy grew in small bunches around the room from cupped ridges that protruded from the walls. "It's a bathroom," he said to Alexa. "There's actually a seat. And, can you believe, it doesn't even smell in here."

"That's always nice," said Alexa. She looked at Krug who had a little smile on his face. "Krug, since we'll be staying the night, would you mind if I took a bath? I'm feeling kind of grimy."

He nodded. "You can wath your clothesth firsth and

lay them on thith rock." He patted his hand on a rock above where the water flowed through. "They will dry fasth from the heat. There ith the barmy leaf over there that you can wath with," he said, pointing at a stack of thick green leaves. Alexa remembered seeing the plant in his garden.

"We'll wait in the other room. I'll watch over Bandit. Holler if you need anything, or if your ears start to tingle. I'll bathe after you," said Aren. He was amazed at how neat and clean the troll was, aside from his snot wiping incident. He never imagined that a troll would have a bathtub, or a toilet for that matter. He wondered how often Krug actually took a bath.

In the living area, Krug rearranged the blankets to cushion the slab before they sat. After getting comfortable, Krug played gently with Bandit tickling his fur while Aren pulled the book from the satchel to study the map. He enlarged the area from Krug's Cave to Dragon Fire wondering which way Krug would lead them. Other than the main trail, the only other way he could see for them to go was along the riverbanks.

"Hey Krug, can you show me on the map which way we will be going?"

"Hmm, you will go thisth way," he said, sliding his finger from Krug's Cave to Dragon Fire.

"But how? Those look like pretty steep mountains, with sheer cliffs."

"You won't gothe over them, you'll gothe through them," he said. "There isth a secret passthage way. It isth very dark, so you'll need a torch. It will take you a lot of hoursth to get to Dragon Fire, so you need to sthart early. It takes youth farther from Retharoths, but ith should be the safeth way."

"So, there's a tunnel?"

"Yesth. It gesth very hot and sthicky in the tunnel. The closther you get to Dragon Fire, the warmer it getsth. It isth easthy to get losth if you don't know your way. The tunnel goesth in different directions in stheveral placeths, but if you alwaysth follow the main flow, you will be okay." He tickled Bandit again. "In sthome parts it gets pretty wet, too. This isth the seasthon when the water isth flowing high, so the main path may be flooded about mid-way there. You willth need to take the water-bowl the resth of the way."

"What's a water-bowl?"

"Itsth a big bowl that floasth on the water." He used his hands to show its shape. "You sith in it."

"Oh, you mean a boat?"

"Uh, well, itsth a bowl. Ith will take you to the dragon's teeth. That is where you havth to climb out and then crawl through the teeth."

"How will you get the bowl back?"

Krug shrugged his shoulders.

"Are there any dangerous creatures in the tunnel?"

"I do noth think so. Although, mosth that have entered Dragon Fire have never come out. They stheem to all disthappear."

"Uh, okay. Well, how do we get through it and out safely?"

"Oh, thasth easthy," he said, chuckling with a wave of his hand. "When you geth to the Heart of the Dragon, remember, do noth try to touch the heart! You can climb acrossth the dragon's teeth and out of the cave. Ith can be a little tricky because the teeth geth wet from the stheam that risthes from the water. Whatever you do, do noth touch the water! Ith is lava hot! If you fall in, you will die immediately."

"What is the Heart of the Dragon? And why do so many disappear?"

"It isth the dragon's egg that she wasth protecting when she wasth killed. When she died, she wasth sthill holding the egg in her clutchesth. In time, her body and bonesth petrified, encasthing the egg in the cavity of her frame. Her petrified body hollowed on the insthide, forming the cave of Dragon Fire. The dragon'sth fire sthill burnsth from the egg that livesth, heating the water around ith. The water flowsth in from the river through her fangs, keeping it safe from anyone who would try to stheal ith. The mouth of the cave isth literally her mouth." He pointed to his mouth, exposing his teeth. "Her fangsth plunged into the ground leaving narrow gapsth that you can go through to enter the cave. But, the few that hath entered the cave to try to stheal the egg hath never come out. They probably fall into the water and die," he said, matter-of-factly.

"Wow, that's crazy!" Aren said. "Could the egg ever hatch?"

He shrugged his shoulders, and said, "I dunno. Maybe."

"What about Inserpia? Does she ever go in the tunnel?"

"I donth think there is any way for her to geth in there. Itsth too hot through Dragon Fire. The rest of the water flows from underground or through holes that are too small for her big ugly headths." He scrunched up his face, twisting his mouth, making himself look ridiculously ugly.

Aren chuckled. "Okay, I guess we won't worry about that ugly two-headed beast then."

While Krug was playing with Bandit, Aren was studying the map. He enlarged the area around Rheyaros. A small blue circle that he hadn't noticed before caught his attention. Spreading his fingers across the spot of blue to enlarge it as big as he could, he wondered if it was the Skylar Moon.

In the bathing room, Alexa was soaking her weary body in the nice hot bath. It felt like a spa with the hot water streaming and bubbling over her skin. She had first washed her clothes with the barmy leaves, impressed with how clean they had gotten. Her jeans had been gritty and stiff from the caked on dirt, but now they looked as clean as when she had first put them on the day before. After laying her clothes out on the rock to dry, she eased herself into the tub. Scrubbing herself from head to toe with a leaf, she was amazed at the amount of suds it produced. Just one leaf was enough to scour herself clean. Figuring her clothes needed a little more time to dry, she decided to relax and enjoy her bath. After all, she wasn't sure how long it would be before she got the chance to take another one. Her mind started to drift as she leaned her head back and closed her eyes. She wasn't sure how long she had been there before she was jolted awake at the sound of Aren's voice.

"Are you okay in there?" Aren yelled.

"Yes, I'm fine," she yelled back, squirming to sit upright, covering herself with her arms. "Don't come in here, I'm not dressed!" Then she said to herself, “Oh my gosh, I think I fell asleep.”

"I won't come in. You've just been in there an awful long time."

"Sorry. I'm coming out now," she said. She jumped out of the water, then used her hands to squeegee her body off. She twisted the water out of her hair then combed through it with her fingers. Grabbing her clothes, she couldn’t believe that they were completely dry. It felt good to be clean again.

Aren was wielding the sword in the air, getting a feel of it as Alexa walked into the living room area. "Your chin looks better," Aren noticed.

"Good! It feels better."

Aren reluctantly put the sword away, and walked towards the bathing room. "I'll try not to take as long."

"Good luck with that. It's really relaxing," she said.

"Yell if your ears start to tingle," he said.

Chapter Fourteen

"Aren! Wake up! Wake up!"

"What? What's happening?" he asked.

"My ears are starting to tingle." Alexa held her hair back exposing her ears.

With sleepy eyes Aren peered at their redness.

Just then, Krug came running into the living room huffing and puffing. "They are coming! Quick! Follow me," he said, stomping toward the bathing room.

Aren grabbed for his belt and sword, fumbling to put them on as he followed behind Alexa. She had grabbed the satchel and held onto it until he was ready.

"They are still a little waysth away, but riding sthwiftly," Krug explained, as he pushed with his shoulder against a huge boulder that made up a wall inside the bathing room. Grunting as he labored, he managed to say, "I heard their beaststh hoovesth echoing in the canyon. It won't be long before they get here. Aarrgghhh." Columns of dirt fell on Krug's head as the boulder scraped along the ceiling. "Grab a torch!" With each push, the ground crunched as the boulder rolled, inch by inch, until the opening was finally wide enough for Aren to squeeze through. Krug knew if Aren could fit, then Alexa would have no problem. "Quickly! Go!

Remember, follow the main water flowth!"

"Thank you Krug! Thank you for everything!" Aren said, patting Krug on the shoulder as he entered the tunnel.

Before stepping through the archway, Alexa wrapped her arms around Krug, then on tip-toes, she reached up and kissed his leathery cheek. "Thank you Krug. Hopefully, we'll see you again soon," she said.

Bandit popped out of Alexa's pocket onto her shoulder, squeaking as he bounced up and down a couple of times while looking at Krug, then dropped back into her pocket.

"Soon," was all Krug could manage to say. He was sad to see them go and hoped they could not see how choked up he was. "Goodbye my friendsth," he said, as he pushed the boulder back in place.

As soon as the boulder was returned to its original spot, Krug lumbered through the maze of his home as quickly as he could to get outside before the Xendors rode up. He had just stepped outside and picked up his stirring bone, pretending to be inspecting the crack, picking at it with his finger nail, when the Xendors rounded the corner. The three of them came to a halt in line formation in front of him once again.

Krug looked up at them and growled.

"Good morning, Krug," Odin said curtly. "Do you have any news for me?"

Krug noticed that Odin and his men looked haggard as if they had ridden all night and hadn't slept. Dark circles had formed under their eyes since seeing them just yesterday. *Good,* thought Krug, *they'll not have as much energy if it comes to a fight.* "I havth nothing for you!"

Glendon, the Xendor that had threatened Krug the day before, drew his sword and nudged his horse towards Krug.

Odin reached his arm out to stop him. "Not now!" His voice was stern, commanding his obedience.

"I'll slash his big ugly head in half! Just let me at him!" Glendon snapped. His stringy blond hair fell in front of his eyes, but it did not cover the hatred he had for the troll.

"Some other time," Odin said, annoyed at his sentry. "Krug, what is it that you have all over your hair?"

Krug bent and shook his head. Dust and pebbles that had littered his hair from the ceiling rained down. *How do I explain that?* he thought. Then he saw the rock on the ground that he had smashed with the bone. He pointed at the rock with the bone, then said, "I had an unexpectheted visitor who refusthed to leave. He was insisthent on being my guesth for dinner. You understhand what I'm sthayin'?" He smiled crookedly, as he nodded towards his cooking pot.

Odin looked down at the broken rock, and then at the pot, wondering what creature was stupid enough to wander into Krug's domain and expect to live through it. "So, you haven't seen any children then?" Odin asked.

"Like I saith before, they would be sthewing in my pot!" Krug lied.

"Very well." Odin turned his mount, but as he did, he again stared into the cave. It was pitch black, impenetrable to the eye. He looked back over his shoulder and saw Glendon, with his sword held high, urge his horse toward Krug. Odin spun around and yelled, "I said not now!" Odin did not want to risk losing any of his men while searching for Aren and Alexa. He would hate to have to explain that to Mara. Although Glendon was a very capable swordsman, he wasn't sure he would win his hand at battle with the troll.

Glendon reined in his horse as he stared at Krug who held the bone across his chest in a stance ready to fight. Their eyes battled in a stare-out until Glendon had to break off and turn to ride, following Odin's command.

Krug did not relax his stance until the Xendors were well on their way. When he could no longer see them, he tossed the bone over his shoulder then lumbered over to the rock at the entrance to the cave and sat heavily. He closed his tired eyes, which were heavy from lack of sleep. Determined to keep Aren and Alexa safe, he had stayed awake all night keeping watch. At the break of dawn, he had crept through the canyon to its highest peak, looking and listening for any signs of the Xendors and their horses. As he expected, they had come back after their search beyond the canyon had proved fruitless. As soon as he had heard the sound of hoof beats, he ran as quickly as he could back to his cave to warn Aren and Alexa.

The boulder to the hidden passageway was harder to move than he had anticipated, probably from not having been moved in years, but he was determined to get them through. His body now ached from having pushed the weight of the boulder, but it was a good ache, an ache earned from doing a good deed. He wished that their mother would visit soon so he could let her know that her children had been here, and where they were now headed. Fearing the Xendors, or the witch Mara, would find them first made his stomach turn. He decided to push aside the worrisome thoughts, and instead filled his mind with memories of his beloved Kreega as he drifted off into a deep sleep.

Chapter Fifteen

As Emma was getting ready to enter the library Tara caught up to her. "Hey, Emma. Wait up."

"Oh, hi Tara."

"Hey, did you get the chance to talk to Aren last night?" Tara asked.

Emma hugged her books and shook her head. "No. Did you?" She didn't want to reveal that her dad would never allow her to call a boy. He didn't think it was proper. Trying to explain to him why she would have the need to call a boy would have been more trouble than it was worth, and she didn't want to lose her chance at going to the dance. She was sure her dad didn't understand a thing about kids these days, but she wasn't about to school him on the subject since he thought he knew everything there was to know about everything, and more. Her dad was the one thing she feared more than anything else in the world.

"No, I haven't talked to either of the A-twins. Neither has Josh nor Dain," Tara said.

"Maybe Allison has," Emma suggested.

"Actually, she hasn't heard from them either. But, she is working attendance in the office today, so maybe she'll be able to find out what's going on."

"Oh, good."

"Hey, do you have to go to the library, or can you hang out with us?" Tara asked.

"Um, sure. I can hang out," Emma said.

"Great! Come on. There's Josh and Dain." Tara tucked her arm through Emma's, guiding the way.

"How can you eat that junk?" Dain was scolding Josh as Emma and Tara slid on the bench across from them.

"It's easy. Like this, you dip it, then pop it in your mouth, then chew," Josh said, demonstrating how to properly eat a spicy cheese puff dipped in ranch dressing. "Mmmm." His jaw moved with exaggerated chews.

"That's disgusting. No wonder you're so fat," Dain said.

Emma was surprised at how brutally guys could talk and joke with each other. She could never imagine saying those things to another girl. If anyone ever said anything like that to her the way Dain said it to Josh, she would probably run off in tears.

"I'm not fat. I'm pleasantly plump. More of me to love." Josh smiled. He popped another dripping cheese puff into his mouth.

Allison joined the group. "Hey guys! Guess what?" Before they could respond to her, she asked, "Ew, Josh, what are you eating?"

"Spicy cheese puffs dipped in ranch dressing. Want

some?"

"Gross! No! That can't be good for you."

"Hey, don't knock it before you try it. It's delish!" he boasted, then popped another one in his mouth.

Allison shook her head and bit her tongue to keep herself from saying what she really thought about the disgusting snack.

"Did you find out about the A-twins?" Dain asked, changing the subject.

"Yes. But, it's rather sad," Allison said, averting her eyes.

"Well, what is it? Are they okay?" Tara asked.

"Well, the A-twins are okay, I guess you could say," Allison said.

The suspense was eating at Emma. She wished Allison would just spit it out and tell them what was going on. She didn't want to appear too impatient so she sat quietly and waited, hugging her books.

"Then what is it? How come they aren't here?" Dain asked.

"I hate to be the one to deliver such bad news," Allison said somberly, shaking her head.

"What?!" they all said at once.

"It's Nana, their grandma. Apparently, she passed away on Monday."

"Oh no! That's so sad," Tara said. "She was such a

nice lady."

"I overheard the principal saying that the services were private and being held out-of-town," Allison added.

They all looked down, not knowing what else to say or do. None of the kids knew that Nana Gazelle wasn't really Aren and Alex's grandma, they just assumed so because of her name.

Emma's heart was breaking for Aren and Alexa, *and herself.* Having had lost someone very dear recently, she thought she knew what they must be feeling right now. The hollowness returned to the pit of her stomach at the memory of her mother. She felt extremely selfish because her sadness at the moment wasn't just for Aren and Alexa, or for having lost her own mother, it was because her one chance of happiness in high school was now gone. Her dream of going to the dance with Aren, was just that, only a dream. Ashamed that she was feeling such self-pity during a time where she should be thinking only of Aren and Alexa, she felt tears start to well up in her eyes. Absorbed in her own selfish thoughts, she did not hear what the others had been talking about.

"Well, what do you think Emma?" Allison asked. They were all looking at her now.

"Um, I'm sorry. I wasn't listening. What do I think about what?" she said, wiping at her eyes trying to keep the tears from falling.

Tara patted Emma's shoulder gently as if to say she understood her sadness.

"We were thinking of all pitching in and donating to a cause in memory of their grandma. What do you think?" Allison asked.

"Oh. I think that is a great idea. I'm sure they would like that very much." Two separate thoughts invaded Emma's mind at once. She remembered feeling grateful at the thoughtfulness of others when the local animal rescue center notified her father that several people had donated gifts in memory of her mother. The other thought going through her mind was where she was going to get the money from to pitch in. She wouldn't dare ask her father. That might cause him to go on a tangent about her mother. What her father didn't know was that her mother had a stash of money hidden away under a floorboard in Emma's room that she was planning on using to move the two of them far away from him. But, her untimely death came just weeks before their planned departure. Emma decided to keep the money hidden until she graduated from high school, and then she would use it to leave without telling her father where she was going. She would be eighteen by then, and legally able to leave if she chose to. She thought about how her mother might feel if she took a little money for a situation such as this, and decided she probably wouldn't mind at all.

"Anyone have any ideas what cause we should give to?" asked Allison.

Both the boys shrugged their shoulders.

Emma suggested, "How about the animal rescue center?"

"That's a great idea!" agreed Tara. "Everyone loves animals."

"Works for me," said Dain.

"Me too," said Josh.

"Great! Then the animal rescue center it is," said Allison. "Let's not put a limit on what each of us pitch in. Just pitch in whatever you can. Okay?"

They all agreed.

"Okay, bring whatever it is you want to donate not later than Friday, and I can take it to the shelter after school. Then we can present it to the A-twins either Saturday before the dance if they are still going, or Sunday, or whenever we see them again," said Allison.

"Do you think they'll still be going to the dance?" Emma asked, trying not to sound too hopeful.

"Maybe. Right now, they are out of town with family according to their attendance report. They may not feel up to going, which would be totally understandable, since this just happened on Monday," said Allison.

"Will you still be going Emma?" Dain asked, while running his fingers through his tussled hair.

"I ... I'm not sure. Well, actually, I, um, yes. I'll still be going." She wasn't sure if she should tell them that Aren had invited her to the dance.

"Okay, good!" Dain said.

"Unless the A-twins need us for something, I'll still be going," said Tara.

"Me too," said Allison.

"Me three," said Josh. They all rolled their eyes at him.

"I'll be there," said Dain. "Here Allison," he said, handing her a wadded up bill. "I won't be here for the rest of the week, so here is my contribution."

"Oh, that's right. Thanks." Allison tucked the bill in the side pocket of her backpack.

Emma tried to pay attention and participate in the conversation with the group, but she found it hard because her mind kept wandering to Aren and the dance. *Please, please, be back in time for the dance. All I really want is to dance with you, Aren, just once! And then I will be happy, and no one can take that moment of happiness away from me no matter what. Not my father, not anyone. Please.*

They all stood up to return to class when the bell rang. Dain and Josh headed in one direction and the three girls in another.

As they neared their classroom, Allison said, "So, if any one of us hears from either one of the twins do we all agree to let each other know right away?"

The three agreed.

"Okay, good. I'll say something to Josh and Dain, too, but as soon as they agree to keep us up-to-date on any important news, you know they will forget, and insist we never even talked about it," Allison said shaking her head.

"Boys!" Tara rolled her eyes. "They can't be trusted."

They chuckled, then parted ways, and went into their classes.

Chapter Sixteen

Its name meant something that had to do with love, he remembered Mara telling him. But as he sat upon his horse at the edge of Wooer's Peak and looked below at the panoramic view of Noki Lake, it made Odin think of nothing more than a person's entrails. The main inlet that fed into the pear shaped body of the lake swirled in a gush of water like liquid passing through an esophagus, and into the cavity of a stomach. From there, white-capped ripples swept their way across the deep blue stomach of the lake to the opposite shore, lapping upon a sandy beach. With the dunes of the beach on one side, and the edge of the forest on the other, the start of a long winding river twisted itself like intestines from the lake, through the forest of Vesterra, finally spewing its contents into the vast waters of the Kamari Sea.

"Will we be resting here?" Glendon asked Odin hopefully.

"No," he said.

"But Sir, our horses need rest and ..." Glendon did not finish his sentence before Odin cut him off.

"We'll rest by the water where our horses can drink and feed on the reeds," he said. "Let's move."

They rode in silence through the trees until Odin

declared a spot fit for them to stop. "We'll rest here."

Both his men dismounted their horses, moaning as they stretched their backs and legs. They flopped to the ground and sprawled out in exhaustion.

Odin looked at them with disgust. “I've chosen two wimps, I see!” He dismounted, also feeling the strain in his legs and back from sitting on his horse for so long. Looking down on his men, he thought that being younger, they should be less sore than him, with more energy, but apparently not. They already appeared to have fallen asleep. He figured he would make men of them eventually. He kicked one in the boot, startling him awake.

"Huh? What?" Glendon grumbled, confused as he bolted upright.

"Both of you," he kicked Drexter next, "take this time to eat. Regain some strength."

"I'm too tired to eat," complained Drexter, rolling over onto his side, never opening his eyes.

"Me too," said Glendon. "We've ridden for nearly two days without stopping. Might we rest just a bit?"

"We have no time to be tired," Odin said.

His sentries groaned, but still made no attempt to get up.

Odin decided to let them rest for fear that they'd likely fall asleep on their horses. *Worthless fledglings.* Odin walked away from them, letting them sleep. He retrieved some food from his saddle pack and sat against a tree to eat his meal, watching as their horses eagerly lapped up water as if they would drink the lake dry. He supposed they need their rest, too.

By the position of the sun Odin knew half the day was gone, but with the horses watered and fed, they should be able to make Pellyn by nightfall, even with a rest. He wondered where Aren and Alexa could be. They had found no sign at all of the two. No foot prints, no litter, no nothing. The elves they had seen were not acting suspicious. They didn't appear to be trying to hide anything, they were acting normal with no signs of disruption. Not surprisingly, there were no sightings of the Faeries. The Gnomes of Girk were scared out of their minds when the three Xendors rode upon them, disrupting their tinkering. They were always making some sort of trinket with rocks and remnants that littered the ground. Odin was certain he had properly persuaded the gnomes to send for him if any of them caught sight of the two kids. Inserpia had been too active to have encountered the two. After a feasting, she would remain docile for several days while her body digested its food, so, he was sure she hadn't found them. And Krug, as insolent as ever, could not be trusted. Would he really stew the kids in his pot? Odin didn't think so, but, with a troll, you never know.

Chapter Seventeen

"Still no word," Harbin announced regretfully to Yasmin.

Yasmin's worried look turned to determination. "Please, Harbin, have our horses ready for us. Erik and I will be riding out shortly." Her voice was calm, disguising the torment of emotions that were whirling inside of her.

"My Lady, would you like some of our men and me to ride with you?" Harbin asked.

"No, but thank you, Harbin. We will be fine. Erik and I want to give the appearance that we are out for a casual ride, such as we often do. If Mara's heathens see us with a company, it will raise their suspicion and cause them to follow us, which they will probably do anyway. But, please continue to have the guards do as they have been instructed. We still don't want to draw attention to Rheyaros. Without the sword in place, we are too vulnerable."

"How soon shall the horses be ready?" Harbin asked.

"Erik will be here momentarily, then we will depart."

Harbin noticed Yasmin was already dressed in her casual riding attire and thought he should suggest she change into safety gear for added protection. "Ma'am, considering the circumstances, may I please suggest you wear a more protective ensemble?"

"Thank you for your concern, Harbin." Yasmin smiled sweetly at him. "I had Sara alter my casuals last night. My clothes have been insulated with a layer of safety leather." She thought she would try to make light of the situation and patted her hips with her hands, "didn't you notice the extra weight I was carrying around?"

"Uh," was all that emitted from Harbin's slack-jawed mouth. He knew Yasmin was teasing him. Although, he had noticed she looked a bit thicker, he knew better than to ever mention weight gain to a female ever again. Not too long ago, he had learned his lesson after he made the mistake of asking Sara if she was with child when he noticed she had been gaining a bit of weight around her mid-section. She had slapped his face in disgust and left him standing there in shock. At the time, he wasn't sure what he had said that warranted that kind of reaction. He had always thought Sara was too skinny, and liked the way she looked with the few added pounds. Later, he had discovered she was trying to bulk up in hopes that he would pay more notice to her. Before then, he had no idea that she'd ever been interested in him. Ever since the face slapping incident, he had been trying to repair the damage he caused in their friendship, but she was playing hard to get and being very coy with him. Unfortunately, Harbin did not have time at the present to invest in trying to win her affection. He had to put all his personal problems aside and focus his full attention on his duties. After the night of the Skylar Moon, he would try again with Sara. *No! Not try! I will succeed in winning her affection,* he thought whole heartedly.

Yasmin knew of the incident involving Sara and felt a tinge of guilt teasing Harbin. Rarely has an elf of his age had to shoulder the amount of responsibility that he has. After the attack on their people, many of the elder elves were killed or maimed, leaving the burden of leading and protecting their people to many of the young and inexperienced. Harbin's intelligence, along with his will and determination, quickly earned him the roll as Arch Guard, the top elf in charge of their defenses. She knew that his duties were his top priority and that he took them very seriously, which was why he was so good at what he did. But still, she thought, an elf as young as he should be able to experience the happiness of being in love. She hoped that he soon would be afforded that opportunity, as soon as her people were once again safe.

Chapter Eighteen

They walked cautiously through the cave, unable to avoid stepping in the little puddles and streams of water that crossed the path along the underground river. Alexa was grateful that the hiking boots she wore were waterproof, keeping her feet dry.

"I feel as if we've been walking for hours," Alexa said. Her voice echoed as it bounced off the walls.

"We have," confirmed Aren.

Throughout most of the cave, the water flowed swiftly, but at this particular juncture, it stilled in an oval pool. The light from the torch was not enough for them to see the bottom, so they had no idea if it was deep or not. A drop of water fell from a slow drip through a crack in the ceiling, plopping loudly into the pool. As soon as the ripples faded, another droplet would fall and start the pattern over. Alexa watched the ripples as memories of Inserpia assaulted her mind. She shivered at the thought.

"What if Inserpia appears?"

"Krug said she can't get in here." Aren's eyes wandered, looking for places where Inserpia might be able to edge her way in.

"Why not?"

"The only way in is through Dragon Fire, and that's too hot for her big ugly heads, according to Krug." Aren smirked at the memory of the face Krug had made when he described Inserpia.

They continued on to the opposite end of the pool, where the water branched out in three different directions. Walking along the path, they were grateful to find they were on the side with the main water flow, and did not have to cross over to the other channels.

"Do you think we're close?" Alexa asked.

"Well, Krug said that half-way there we would find a water bowl that we would need to take the rest of the way to Dragon Fire. Since we haven't seen a water bowl, I'd say no, we are not almost there."

Alexa grunted, then asked, "What's a water bowl?"

"According to Krug, it's a bowl that you sit in on the water. I'm guessing it is similar to a boat."

"Hmm. Well, I'm getting hungry. Do you think we could find a place to rest for a bit and eat a wafer?" she asked.

"That's the best idea you've had all day!" exclaimed Aren.

"It's the only idea I've had all day," Alexa giggled.

They found a dry outcrop of rock against the wall of the cave to sit on. Handing Alexa the torch, Aren took the tube of wafers from the satchel. Opening it, he gave one to her.

She quickly stuffed it in her mouth chewing eagerly thinking about how hungry she was. Just then, Bandit popped out of her pocket and sat upon her leg staring up at her. His eyes glowed golden against the torch light. She stopped in mid-chew remembering he needed to eat also. Pinching a tiny piece of the wafer from her mouth, she offered it to Bandit. "I'm sorry little guy. I almost forgot about you. Do you want this?" she asked.

Bandit appeared to sniff at it, but made no attempted to take it.

"Maybe he doesn't like regurgitated food." Aren crinkled his nose, and smiled.

She nudged her fingers toward him trying to get him to take the piece. "I was so hungry, I didn't even think about giving any to him," she said, swallowing the wafer. "I feel so bad. He won't take it."

Aren laughed. "I'll give him some of mine. Here Bandit." He broke off a tiny piece of the wafer offering it to him.

Bandit sniffed at the offering, then his tongue jutted out and snatched up the morsel. He belched, causing Aren and Alexa to chuckle at his cuteness.

"What's this?" Alexa said to Bandit, noticing a small piece of cloth sticking out from under him. She held it close to her eyes, inspecting it in the dim light, as Bandit jumped up and down on her leg making a little squeaking sound.

"What? Where did you get this?" she asked Bandit, looking at him then at the little piece of cloth. It looked familiar, but it wasn't from any of their clothing.

"Let me see it," Aren said.

Bandit jumped to Aren's lap and bounced up and down letting out several squeaks.

"Here, you can have it back." Aren handed him the piece of cloth.

With one of his tiny feet, Bandit snatched the cloth and tucked it under his fur. With it secure, he jumped back onto Alexa's lap, then scurried up her shirt and back into her pocket.

"I think that was a piece of Krug's blanket," Aren said.

"Why would he take a piece of Krug's blanket?"

"Um, because he's a thief. Remember?"

Alexa pulled open her pocket and looked at Bandit. "Did you take a piece of Krug's blanket?"

He kept his eyes downcast as if he was ashamed for pilfering the piece of cloth.

Alexa thought on it a moment. She felt bad for Bandit. He seemed to be embarrassed at being caught taking something that didn't belong to him. "Bandit, did you want to keep a little reminder of Krug? Is that why you took a piece of his blanket?" she asked.

Bandit's sad eyes widened making them look too

large for his tiny body. He rubbed at the cloth with his toes.

"Don't worry Bandit. I'm pretty sure Krug won't mind that you took a little memento to remember him by." Alexa stuck her finger in her pocket and gave Bandit a little rub on the top of his head until he started to purr. "He would probably feel a little flattered."

"Krug will probably never notice the piece missing anyway. Those blankets were pretty ragged," Aren said.

"True. But, Bandit shouldn't make a habit of just taking things from anyone. He should learn to ask."

"And how do you suppose he could do that? Just say, Hey Krug! Mind if I swipe a piece of your blanket to remember you by?" Aren teased.

"Very funny, Aren."

They decided not to sit for too long since they had no idea how much farther they had to go. Aren figured they had been walking for about four or five hours through the cave already. It was hard to tell since there was no outside light to guide them through the day. Krug had been correct about the cave getting more humid, and so far, they hadn't come across any creatures.

They walked a couple more hours before Alexa said, "Dang, I feel as if we have been walking forever. Does this cave ever end? Are we even sure we're going the right way?"

"Well, we've been following the main waterway, so we must be going the right direction, according to Krug.

Hopefully, the bowl will be around here somewhere." As soon as Aren finished saying it, he noticed a huge wooden bowl leaning against the wall. "Look!" he exclaimed. "The bowl!"

"And just in time too! The path is starting to get really narrow," Alexa pointed out.

"Okay, how are we going to do this?" Aren asked, assessing their circumstances.

"Well, since there isn't any room to step around the bowl, only one of us is going to be able to lower it into water. Do you think you will be able to do that, and hold it against the current long enough for me to get in, then you can jump in?" Alexa suggested.

"We'll find out. Get ready to jump in," he said, handing the torch to Alexa. Aren reached for the top of the bowl pulling it away from the wall. As it hit the water, he stumbled and almost lost his grip on the smooth edges. The bowl started to slip from his grasp, but his hand caught hold of a handle that was carved on the inside. He held on tight and braced himself. He was trying to keep it steady though it felt as if it was going to rip from his hands. "Quick! Get in!" he yelled to Alexa.

She nudged up next to him, then jumped, landing awkwardly against the other side. Aren tumbled in after her with his feet hanging over the edge. They both righted themselves and sat up on their knees. There were no seats.

"Wow, this really is a bowl," Aren said, as it spun with the current. "Is Bandit okay?"

"Yup. He's safe and dry in my pocket." Alexa wiped at a splash of water that sprinkled her face.

"Good. Now be on the lookout for huge teeth. That will be our exit point."

"How far do you think it is?" she asked.

"Probably not for a while. Krug said the bowl was half-way."

Aren was relieved to discover a notch carved inside the bowl that was a perfect fit for holding the torch. His arm needed the rest, and so did Alexa, apparently. They hadn't traveled far before the gentle sway of the bowl rocked her to sleep.

Chapter Nineteen

Thunk . . . thunk . . . thunk . . .

"Huh," Aren sat up with a start. He shook off the groggy feeling clouding his head. *Oh no! I must have fallen asleep,* he thought. They were caught in an eddy cornered between a row of pillars and the wall of the cave. "Alexa, wake up!"

"What? What's going on?" Alexa forced her eyes to open.

"Apparently we both fell asleep. Now we're stuck in a slow spin in a corner here. I'll need your help pushing us out."

"Oh man. Okay, what do you want me to do?" she asked, wiping sweat from her forehead.

"Well, I'm going to grab onto one of these pillars to try and stop us from spinning, then if you can grab onto one of those pillars," Aren pointed at the last two pillars next to a flat rock, "we'll try to pull ourselves out of the eddy."

"Um, Aren," Alexa said.

"What?"

"Do you notice anything strange about these pillars?" She pointed at their shape.

Aren's gazed traveled up and down. "What? That they're white, like ivory, and not like the normal stalagmites that form in a normal cave? Remember, we're in Vesterra. Nothing is normal here."

"Exactly!" Alexa nodded her head. "And, the cave is brighter! Notice the light filtering in through the pillars?"

"Oh my gosh! You're right! Dragon Fire! We must be at Dragon Fire!" he exclaimed, his eyes wide with excitement. "No wonder it's so hot and humid. I'm dripping in sweat. Let's try to stop the bowl so we can look through the pillars, or ... teeth. I think these are the dragon's teeth, or fangs, or whatever it is that dragons have!"

"But they're really close together," Alexa noticed. "Maybe we can push our way to those flat rocks. We should have a clear view from there, if we can steady the bowl and climb on top of them."

"I think those rocks are probably molars." Aren grabbed onto one tooth, stopping the bowl from turning.

Alexa reached her hand between the tightness of two teeth, then they both started to pull. The eddy was strong, testing their combined strength. Soon, the bowl dipped and they moved along. Alexa bypassed the first molar and grabbed onto the second one.

"Can you climb up?" Aren asked.

"Yep! Hang on." Alexa reached her hand over the top of the tooth, and using the edge of the bowl for foot support, she pulled herself up and onto the molar. She gasped at the sight before her.

It wasn't until Aren yelled, "a little help here please," that Alexa realized Aren was still in the bowl. He grunted, trying to hold on so the bowl wouldn't drift away with him in it.

"Oh, sorry," Alexa said, forcing her eyes from the amazing spectacle. She laid on her stomach reaching over the edge to hold the rim of the bowl. Once Aren hefted himself up, Alexa released the bowl letting it float away.

Resting on his knees, he stared in wonderment. "Whoa! Look at that!"

Before them loomed the Heart of the Dragon. Protectively clutched atop an island of petrified bones that had once been the dragon's claws was a magnificent egg. The skeletal phenomenon sat like a haunting exhibit on display in the mist of scalding water that percolated around it.

"Aren look! The egg! Do you see the light?" Alexa pointed at the center of the egg.

"Yes! I bet it's alive! Just like Krug thought it might be!"

Marbled with different shades of green, the egg pulsated with a faint light to the beat of a concealed heart.

"That's amazing," Alexa said. "I can't believe there could really be something still alive in that egg."

"Seriously! I wonder what would happen if it actually hatched."

"Well, if it's still alive, why hasn't it hatched?" Alexa asked, puzzled.

"That is something we'll probably never know. But, I can see why anyone who would try to steal the egg would die. Look how hot the river is." Aren watched the steam as it rose from the bubbling water around the island of bones. "We need to figure out how to get out of here without falling. Krug said we need to walk along the teeth." He looked at the row of teeth to assess their situation. There were crevices at the top that they could grab onto where the teeth protruded from the bone. The bottom teeth were half submerged, and nearly flush with the top teeth, leaving only small gaps where they could place their feet. "Dang, this dragon had some major jaws!" he said, noticing the distance they needed to go, silently wondering if they were going to make it. "It must have been gianormous!"

Alexa smiled at his description. "I'd have to agree. Definitely a gianormous dragon."

A worried look covered Alexa's face. She wasn't sure she was tall enough, with her feet needing the support of the bottom teeth. Normally, she was comfortable with her height, but this was one of those times when being vertically challenged could pose a problem. "Aren, I'm not sure if I can make it."

"Sure you can."

"I'm not that tall. What if I fall?"

"You won't," he said, looking at the size of the teeth. They appeared to be too wide for her to reach around from one to the other, and not enough space for her to walk along the base. She would have to scale across from the top. "How about if I lift you up so you can grab onto the edge of the tooth. Then you can climb across. Think of it as scrambling across a tree branch. That should be a piece of cake for you," he was trying to sound encouraging.

"Um, yea, sure," she said. "Okay, let's get this over with. Give me a boost."

He lifted her with ease as she grabbed onto the gap above the tooth. She slowly started to inch her way across, noticing how sharp the edges were. “Don't look down. Don't look down,” she kept whispering to herself. As she rounded each tooth, she wedged a foot between them for support taking some of the stress off her arms. "These teeth are pretty sharp, and slippery," she said. "Tell me I'm almost there please!"

"You only have three teeth to go! You can do it Lex!"

Just then Alexa screamed, releasing one of her hands.

"Alexa! Hold on!" Aren shouted, as he started his way across.

"Aren! I can't!" She was desperately hanging on by one hand.

"Try to reach back up!"

"I can't! I'm slipping! It's cutting my fingers!" Fear

consumed her.

"Try to wrap your legs around the tooth for support! I'm coming! Hold on!"

Alexa screamed. She swung her legs around the tooth, hugging her knees against it. "Hurry! My hand is slipping!" She tried to pull her body against the tooth, but her position was too awkward.

Aren scurried along on his tiptoes, clutching tight to the top. Merely inches from Alexa, his foot slipped. Lava hot water doused the tip of his shoe sending a wave of heat through his foot. He jerked his leg up nearly causing himself to lose his grip. The pain cutting into his fingers was excruciating, as he scrambled to wedge his foot between two teeth. Barely secure, he reached out with one arm and grabbed Alexa around her waist, pulling her toward him.

In a panic, Alexa flung herself at her brother, wrapping her arms around his neck.

Aren screamed as his body twisted with the force while struggling to hold on to Alexa and the tooth's jagged edge. "Lex I need you to get on my back and hold on around my neck," he shouted. As he reached up, she wiggled her way around him, wrapping her legs around his waist, and her arms around his sweaty neck.

"Are you okay, Lex?" he asked, once she stopped squirming.

"Yes, but I'm scared!" her voice cracked.

Okay, hold on tight. I'm going to get us out of here." He moved with caution across the teeth. His arms and back ached from the weight of his sister.

"Only two more teeth to go, then we'll be out!" Alexa tried to sound encouraging.

Aren grunted as he inched along, trying to ignore the increasing pain radiating in his hands and arms. He could feel the wet stickiness of blood around his fingers.

"One more tooth!" Alexa announced.

Aren positioned himself so Alexa could land on a small pad of dirt embedded with a lone fang. She leapt to the ground, then squirmed her way through the gap in the teeth, falling on her hands and knees outside of the cave. Aren followed suit, collapsing next to his sister, taking in deep breaths, relishing the fresh air.

Chapter Twenty

Something wet and gritty rubbed against his cheek. Odin jumped up, flailing his arms to ward off the intruder. He lost his footing as he tripped over an exposed tree root, and tumbled into the lake. The cool water shocked his senses as he staggered to stand. Dripping with water, he spun towards the shore, drawing his sword and slashing it in front of him. He turned his head to and fro but saw nothing, except the three horses, and his two sleeping sentries. He noticed his horse was standing near the tree where he had been resting, and then it donned on him, “Blast it! I had fallen asleep!” His horse cocked its head and puckered out its lips as if laughing at him. That was when he realized it was his steed’s grimy lips kissing his cheek that had woken him. "You worthless mutt!" he said, splashing water at his muzzle. "Look at what you've done! Now I'm soaking wet!" His boots were filled with water making them heavy and hard to walk in as he pushed his way to shore. "I guess I should be thankful," he admitted. "Otherwise, I might have slept all night like those two dolts."

His sentries were snoring loudly, even after all the commotion he had made splashing about. He tossed a handful of water on the sleeping men before exiting the lake.

"Wake up you two! Now!"

They both sat up abruptly, shaking their heads, and wiping their damp faces.

"What's going on?" Glendon asked alarmed, then he looked at Odin in confusion. "Sir, why are you all wet?"

"I decided to go for a swim," he lied. "Might you try it to wake yourselves."

"Uh, I'll pass," Glendon said.

"Me too," said Drexter.

"Suit yourselves. It was quite refreshing."

"Sir, how long have we been asleep?" Drexter asked.

"Too long, clearly. The sun is nearly set. We should have made Pellyn by nightfall. As it stands, we'll be lucky if the moon's light will be bright enough to guide us along the cliffs into the ruins."

"But our horses should have no problem. They see better at night than we do," Drexter reminded him.

Odin nodded in agreement. "Glendon, get a bird ready," Odin commanded. "I suppose we should send word to Mara on our progress."

"You mean lack of progress," Glendon chuckled, while pushing aside the wet strings of blond hair from his eyes.

Odin hefted a heavy slap across Glendon's face with a glove for his insolence.

"Yes, sir." Glendon straightened and immediately went to his pack to withdraw writing utensils. Embarrassed by the blow, he had known better than to verbalize such an insult. Odin had always insisted that failure was not an option for him, nor for the men in his unit. Knowing it was a sensitive subject for Odin, since he had failed in locating the sword, and had recently lost two men, made the wisecrack even worse. Glendon knew he was going to have to be on his best behavior from now on. Proving his allegiance to Odin, and his fervor toward their mission, were important in demonstrating his worthiness as a high-sentry. The last thing he wanted was to be sent back to the wall.

"In your own words, tell Mara that so far there have been no signs of the children. We are now west along Noki Lake, en route to Pellyn in case they are being hidden in the ruins. The east and south check clear."

"Yes, sir."

Odin thought about how much ground they covered, amazed at the strength and speed of the horses. Any ordinary horse would never have been able to travel even half the distance they had in the past two days.

Chapter Twenty-one

She had forgotten about Bandit until he squirmed out of her pocket and jumped up and down on her chest. While she laid on the ground inspecting her fingers he nuzzled up against her neck.

"Oh, dang," said Aren, "I almost forgot about Bandit. I'm glad to see he's okay, and doing better than the both of us." He tore a piece of cloth from the bottom of his shirt and wrapped it around his cut fingers.

"I almost forgot about him, too." Heat flushed her cheeks. "He never moved the whole time I was climbing across the teeth." Alexa sat silent for a minute, petting Bandit as she gazed upon the six teeth that spiked the water. They were gapped like tines of a fork, and curved around to the other side of the riverbed forming the cave's entrance. As she watched the water flow between the narrow openings, she said, "Sorry about what happened in there, Aren."

"Don't worry about it, Lex. Everything turned out fine. We're safe. All is good."

"Well, I ... I freaked out when I touched something slimy. That's why I slipped," she confessed.

Before he could respond, the sound of voices caused them to jump up and spin around.

"Oooohhh." Several little men were standing at the edge of the river. They were staring at Aren and Alexa with wide eyes.

"Uh, hello," said Aren.

The little men bowed at Aren's greeting. Then one stepped forward from the group. "Good late day to you. I am Bondalin Jon Bardolyne, of Girk," he said. He looked at the both of them, then craned his head to look around them at the entrance to Dragon Fire. Awe was evident as his eyes settled back on the twins.

Aren and Alexa looked from one little man to the other. Based on the description Nana had given in her stories, they were sure they had just met some gnomes. All of them were about three feet tall, with multi-colored hair twisted in a pile on top of their heads like soft served ice cream.

"I'm Aren, and this is my sister Alexa."

Bondalin's eyes widened at the realization of who the two were. "Oh my, oh my! You must go, you must. Your presence invades our safety, it does," he said straightforward.

"What? Why?" asked Aren.

While listening to Aren converse with Bondalin, Alexa spied two gnomes sitting next to each other on a low tree branch. Their eyes sparkled with a sinister glow as they looked from Aren and Alexa, then to each other. They clasped their hands together, gave each other a crooked smile, then nodded their heads in a silent agreement. Alexa thought them a bit odd compared to the other gnomes in the group, who all seemed to have a more amiable disposition. She averted her eyes from their stares when another gnome stepped forward.

"Good late day. I am Damure Jon Sengur, of Girk," he spoke in a soft and pleasant voice. A tired smile stretched across his face as he spoke. "Men of Mara are seeking a girl and a boy, such as you. Safe you will not be here, nor will we. Leave swiftly, you must, please. A bridge of logs will lead you across the river to the other side toward your journey's end."

"Uh, okay. Who are Mara's men?" Aren asked, already knowing the answer.

"He who is dreadful and full of hate. Odin, he is. Seeking two, such as you," explained Damure, as all the other gnomes nodded their heads in agreement.

At the mention of Odin's name, Aren tensed with his hand going to the hilt of the sword. "I understand," said Aren. He could sympathize with these small men. They must have been completely terrified of Odin, who most likely threatened their lives. He casually looked to Alexa's ears noticing their normalcy indicating to him that there was no immediate threat nearby. Even so, Aren was eager to leave for he did not want to put the gnomes in any danger. They seemed like such docile little people, except maybe for the two sitting in the tree. He couldn't imagine anyone wanting to bring them harm. "So, where is the log bridge?" Aren asked.

"That way," Damure said, pointing his finger towards the trees. "Scurry, hurry, into the trees. Be gone for we fear for all that be. The path will lead the way."

"Okay, thank you," said Aren, as he and Alexa started toward the path.

"Thank you," said Alexa, as she passed by Damure who extended his hand to her in a friendly gesture. As their hands joined she felt a small object between their palms. The look on his face told her that the thing was being given to her in secret as he slyly transferred it, clasping both of his hands around hers. She casually closed her hand into a fist hiding the small object, then gave him a slight nod.

As Aren and Alexa passed, each gnome said courteously, "Good late day to you. Good bye." They carefully stepped around all the interesting looking knickknacks the gnomes were making from the treasures of the forest.

As they entered the trees, Alexa smiled when she looked back noticing the gnomes had immediately started tinkering as if never interrupted. Her smile faded when she also noticed that the two strange gnomes who were sitting on the tree branch were no longer there. She scanned around in search of them, but couldn't find them.

Once they were out of sight, Alexa looked at the

object in her hand. "A shell?" she whispered.

Bandit jumped from her shoulder onto her hand and sniffed at the little gift. He fingered it with his toe, then scurried up her arm and perched himself back onto her shoulder.

"What?" asked Aren.

"Damure gave me a little shell when he shook my hand. I think he was trying to be secretive about it. I wonder what it means." She turned it around, admiring it. The shell was shiny and smooth, with brown and black swirls that reminded her of a piece of candy.

"Maybe it's a good luck charm."

"Maybe." She tucked it in her shirt pocket for safe keeping.

After they were a distance away where she was sure the gnomes couldn't hear, she asked Aren, "Did you notice those two odd looking gnomes sitting in the tree?"

"Yep. Sure did."

"They were kind of creepy, don't ya think?"

"Yep" Aren agreed.

"When I turned back to look, they were gone. I wonder where they went?"

"My guess is they're going to be the ones to report back to Odin that they saw us," he said. "I wonder what he offered them as a reward?"

"That's kind of scary," Alexa said.

"Tell me immediately at the slightest tingle of your ears. I don't want to be surprised."

"I will," she promised.

They pushed aside the spindly branches that whipped at their upper bodies as they walked along the path that was obviously cleared for shorter people. Had they not been directed by the gnomes, they never would have known it was there. After walking about a mile, the path opened up to a small sandy beach along the river bank. Two narrow logs stretched across the river from either side, meeting in the middle just below the surface of the water.

"Tell me that isn't the log bridge," Alexa said.

"I'm afraid so," confirmed Aren.

"Are we seriously supposed to walk across those logs?" Alexa asked.

"I'm not sure they'll support my weight. They look pretty thin," said Aren.

"It wouldn't be a problem if we were gnomes, but we're not." Alexa frowned.

"I'm not sure if we have any other option." Aren looked up and down the river seeing no other bridge. “Let me look at the map and see what I can find." He removed the book from the satchel. After reading the map, he said, "Well, I guess this is it. This is where we're going to have to cross. Unless we want to travel all the way over here." He showed Alexa the map. "I don't think we have time for that."

Looking out across the water, he said, "It doesn't look that deep, but you never know. Rivers can be very deceiving. Let's look for some sticks to help stabilize ourselves as we walk across."

"Good thing we both know how to swim, just in case," Alexa said.

"Hopefully, we won't have a need to test those skills. You never know what slimy creature may be lurking in the water around here."

Alexa shivered. "Oh, great, thanks for the reminder."

They looked around until they both found sticks thick and sturdy enough to help support them.

"I guess I'll go first," said Alexa. "That'll give us a good idea as to whether or not you'll be walking across or swimming."

"Haha, okay, just be careful."

"Oh. I just thought of something," Alexa said.

"Oh, no! You were thinking? That's scary!" teased Aren.

Alexa rolled her eyes. "You might want to brush the sand with a tree branch or something, so our footsteps won't be seen. That way, no one, namely the Xendors, will know we went this way."

"Good idea!" Aren wondered why he hadn't thought of that. He looked around and found a broken branch near the bank and started sweeping along the sand to eliminate their foot prints.

Alexa stepped on the log giving it a little bounce to test its sturdiness. When it didn't move, her confidence rose slightly as she pushed the stick into the water and took her first cautious step. The river wasn't deep but moved swiftly, tugging at the stick. Before long, she had managed to inch her way to the center where the two logs joined below the water. Positioning the stick in front of her as far as she could reach without losing her balance, Alexa jumped to the other log, swaying slightly when she landed. She realized she had been holding her breath and took a moment to breathe before continuing on. Soon she was across, with only her boots having gotten wet.

She turned to motion for Aren to cross and was surprised to see he was already half way along. He was using the same technique as Alexa, jumping from one log to the other. His landing wasn't as graceful, and he nearly plunged into the water. Fortunately, his stick was strong and sturdy, and was able to hold his weight as his body twisted in an ungainly balancing act. Once stable, he hurried along, placing one foot in front of the other in a race to get to the other side. With just a few feet left to go, Aren jumped to the bank then threw his hands in the air, shouting, "TaDa! The Great Aren Rainz completes his amazing balancing act!"

Alexa rolled her eyes. "Oh, brother!"

"That's right! I'm your brother! Brother from the

same mother!" he laughed.

Alexa smiled and shook her head at her brother's silliness. "Which way, Mr. Amazing?"

"That way," he said, pointing into the trees. "I think."

Taking just a few steps, Alexa turned towards the river with a frightened look on her face.

"What's wrong?" Aren asked.

"My ears!" she said, as a black mound crested the water then disappeared.

Aren pulled at the sword ready for Inserpia. He looked to and fro, but she never reappeared.

"She must be gone." Alexa's voice quivered as she spoke. "My ears are no longer tingling."

"Are you sure?" Aren asked, not taking his eyes off the water.

"Yes. Can we go now? I don't particularly like being near the water." Normally, she loved the water. Swimming was one of her passions. It was the water in Vesterra Alexa didn't like.

Aren turned, still holding the sword. "Come on, let's get out of here." It wasn't until they were well into the trees that he put the sword back into its sheath. "It's getting dark. I guess we should find a place to sleep for the night."

"Okay. I wish we were still with Krug." Alexa crossed her arms in a hug. "I felt safe with him."

"Me too, but we aren't, so let's see what we can find,"

he said, a little more tersely than intended.

They found a group of trees with the concave branches and decided it was as good a place as any.

Chapter Twenty-two

"Thank you Krug," Yasmin said relieved, while giving him a tearful hug.

Krug had told Erik and Yasmin that the children had spent the night hiding out in his cave. By now, they should be well past Dragon Fire, if they made it out alive.

Of course they did. They had to have made it. Yasmin refused to think otherwise.

Yasmin was grateful that the kids did not travel the shorter route on the main path towards Rheyaros, even though Dragon Fire could prove equally dangerous. They would have most likely been captured by the Xendors had they traveled along the path. There was no way Yasmin and Erik could make it to Dragon Fire before early evening the next day with nightfall already here.

They were relieved to hear that Odin and his men had gone in the opposite direction. However, they did encounter two of Mara's other sentries along the way to Krug's. The men had been posted on the main path where they were sitting upon their horses, watching as Yasmin and Erik passed by. No exchange between the parties was made, which confirmed to them that there were more Xendor's waiting in the area. They decided to turn their horses onto a rarely used trail, in the opposite direction from where they were headed. Then, when they were out of sight of the Xendors, they turned and rode through the trees towards their intended destination. They did not want the Xendors to know they were going to see Krug. Although Krug was capable of defending himself against Mara's men, he was no match for Mara.

"Youth can sthay here forth the nighth if youth like," Krug offered.

"Thank you Krug, but we need to head back to Rheyaros and give the news to the guards so they can help us in our search. At least now, we have a general idea of where our kids are." Yasmin wished she could stay and visit, but the circumstances did not allow.

Krug nodded in understanding.

Erik reached out grasping Krug's hand in a heartfelt shake, "You are a good friend, Krug. Thank you for your help. We greatly appreciate all you have done. We must part, though, immediately if we plan to make it back before mid-day." The straight, hard ride from Rheyaros to Krug's would normally take nearly a full day without any obstacles. But, with the Xendors on the trail, they could only hope to get back to Rheyaros just after daybreak with taking an alternate route.

Chapter Twenty-three

Alexa fell asleep with thoughts of Nana. Butterflies turned in her stomach thinking about how much she missed her. Her fondest memories would always be their walks to Ice Lake, and listening to Nana tell her stories. "... *and then he threw the kids into the water," Nana said, demonstrating by pushing both Alexa and Aren into the lake. "Then the two became trapped! Their feet stuck, as the muddy bottom of the lake sucked them in. The sun was beating down on them, burning their heads."*

A hissing wind whipped about them. It slapped at the water causing white capped waves to spray in their faces. They struggled to get free. "Nana help!" Alexa screamed. "I can't breathe! My head, it's burning. Help!" She gagged, as she sucked in gulps of water, trying to breathe. She thought she heard Nana on the shore laughing, but it didn't really sound like Nana's laugh, it sounded like a hyena. "Aren!" Alexa screamed. Blinded by the water that stung her eyes, she couldn't see her brother, but she could hear him choking. A wave splashed her face, in her nose, in her mouth. Her head was on fire, but the water was no relief. She tried to scream, but nothing came out. She tried to free herself from the sucking mud, but couldn't move. It pulled at her, sinking her body lower and lower beneath the surface.

Alexa's eyes popped open. Her heart was pounding in her chest. The fire in her dream burned her ears. She was frozen from fear. The dream seemed so real. Too real. She was crying, she noticed as tears dripped down the side of her face. Then another tear ran along her forehead. The sound of the wind was echoing in her ears, but the leaves were still. She was confused. *How did a tear get on my forehead?* Just then, another tear dropped, and rolled near the corner of her mouth. *Those aren't tears!* she realized. *And that noise isn't wind! And! MY EARS!*

Slowly, she reached for the dagger that was just inches from her hand. She positioned her thumb over the little stone. At the same instant she pulled the dagger out, she pushed hard at the stone. The blade slashed through the air over her head. It hit its target, slicing into Inserpia. A deafening screech reverberated through the air. Blood squirted from the wound, spraying Alexa across the face. Fangs bore down on her. She twisted to the side, and swung the dagger again, and again, cutting and slicing. The sound of vertebrates cracking could be heard as Inserpia's head severed from her body. It hit the branch next to Alexa then landed on the ground with a sickening thud.

Inserpia's remaining head gnashed at the air. She thrashed wildly aiming for Alexa, as the bulk of her body wound around Aren and the tree branch, squeezing the life out of him. He couldn't breathe. He was suffocating.

I have to save him! Panic surged through Alexa. She darted to the side, her leg narrowly missing a lethal attack as Inserpia's fangs pierced deep into the tree branch. The serpent convulsed spastically trying to free herself. Alexa took advantage of the moment, hacking and slicing at her neck like a wild beast. Sinewy flesh ripped apart as Inserpia's head detached. Alexa kicked at the serpent's face, until its fangs dislodged. She watched as it fell to the ground next to its twin.

Alexa bounded to Aren, positioning herself above him trying to lift Inserpia's tightly wound carcass. It was extremely heavy, but she finally managed to push the first layer over the side of the branch allowing Aren enough relief to breathe again. He gasped, laboring to suck in air. He was still trapped, unable to move. The dead weight of Inserpia's remains proved to be too heavy for Alexa to unwind. She decided to use her dagger to hack off sections, careful not to stab Aren. She cut like a maniac and tried not to gag at the stench that filled the air from the exposed innards. With every finished cut, she lobbed another piece of Inserpia to the ground. Once she pitched the piece of Inserpia off that laid across Aren's knees, the rest unwound itself, slipping down the trunk of the tree and landing in a heap on the ground.

"Aren! Aren! Are you okay?" Alexa screamed, straddling him.

"I ..." he sucked in air between each word, "thought ... I ... was ... dead." His eyes became huge, "You're ... bleeding."

"What?" She wiped at her face. Her blood covered hands smeared the splatters of gore, painting her cheeks and forehead red. "It's not my blood," she said, feeling a little nauseous at the sight of so much of it. She tried to wipe her hands clean on her jeans. "I'm okay, really. Are you hurt?"

He shook his head, "Don't ... know."

"Don't try to talk just yet. Give yourself time to catch your breath," she said, as she moved over to the other branch giving him some breathing space. "Bandit!" she screamed, when she noticed he wasn't in her pocket. "Bandit, where are you?" She looked around but couldn't see him in the dark. When she looked down all she could see were the haunting, dead eyes from one of Inserpia's heads staring up at her. Her skin prickled at the sight.

"Eeek."

"Bandit? Is that you? Where are you?" Alexa's eyes searched in the darkness.

He squeaked again.

She glanced towards the sound, and could see only his round eyes that shined from the light of the moon. "Come here little guy." She extended her hands, reaching for him.

He looked at her offered hands, but would not move.

"It's okay. Inserpia is dead now. You don't have to worry."

Fear showed in his eyes, and he backed away when she nudged her hands a little closer.

“I must have blood on my face still.” She wiped off her face with the tail of her shirt, grimacing at the amount of blood that now stained her clothing. Her stomach turned at the sight. Leaning forward, she tried again to coax Bandit, "Come on, it's okay, I promise."

He finally hopped onto her waiting hands. His body shook as she nuzzled him with her nose trying to calm him. From underneath, he held the piece of cloth that he had taken from Krug's blanket. His little toes unfolded it to reveal the small shell the gnome had given Alexa.

"Oh." Alexa looked at him surprised to see the shell. She smiled. "Were you keeping it safe for me?" she asked.

He bounced up and down a couple of times, then tucked away the cloth.

She fingered the little shell toward him. “Please, hold it for me. I trust you to keep it safe.”

He looked up at her, then jumped on the shell, and squirmed around until it was positioned securely inside his fur.

"Is he okay?" Aren croaked.

"He's scared. Are *you* okay?"

"I thought I was a goner. I didn't think you were ever

going to wake up." His voice was raspy.

"Sorry. I was having a bad dream. One that I would have loved to avoid having, to help you sooner."

"Man, am I sore. I can't believe neither one of us heard her. I must have been sleeping hard. I didn't wake up until she had me completely wrapped. And by then, I couldn't talk, or scream, or anything. That was totally freaky!" He shuddered involuntarily. Slowly, he sat up while rubbing at his sore muscles. "Hey, did your ears give you any indication that Inserpia was near?"

"Well, I was having this bad dream, and my head was on fire, but we were drowning in the lake." Her voice was shaking reliving the dream. "I guess my head being on fire was really my ears burning, and the water from the lake that was splashing on my face was really water dripping off Inserpia. I'm glad I woke up. I just wish I would have woken up sooner."

"Well, the good thing is, you *did* wake up. Thanks for saving me Sis," he said, reaching a hand across to her.

She took his hand in hers. Tears filled her eyes. “You could have died.”

"But I didn’t. Come on, help me move over to your branch. We'll sit together until daylight."

She reached over to help him across. He was weak and sore, but otherwise seemed unharmed. He sat up with his back against the trunk of the tree and his legs stretched out on the branch. He patted the space next to him for Alexa to sit.

"Are you sure? I have blood all over me from that beast," she said, looking down at her shirt.

"I'm sure." He patted the branch again.

Once she was next to him, he pulled her in, wrapping his arm around her shoulder. Together they sat, silently, until the light of day peaked through the trees.

Chapter Twenty-four

They had ridden all night scouring the dark ruins of Pellyn for any sign of the twins. Odin was starting to feel discouraged that they were unable to find even the slightest trace of them. How was he going to explain this to Mara? But, it wasn't as if Vesterra was a small territory. It was quite large with no easy way to get from one place to another. Surely she would understand how two kids could be hidden so well from them. If it wasn't for his horse, he would never have managed to cover as much ground as he had. After several days of pushing hard, he could tell that even his horses were starting to tire.

As they were exiting the ruins, he noticed a bird circling above his head. At first, he thought the bird an annoyance, and considered lashing at it with his sword. Then he noticed a small note attached to its leg, and wondered if it was a reply from Mara. He stopped and held out his arm allowing the bird to land on it. He untied the note, then let the bird fly away. The coloring and texture of the paper was unfamiliar to him. He carefully unrolled it noticing it was a leaf. His heart skipped a beat when he saw the scratchy, uneven writing: *News we have. At Corbex Clearing we meet at rise of the Sun.*"

It was early morning when Odin and his men rode into the marshland of Corbex Clearing. He immediately saw the two gnomes on the far side, sitting astride a boar. The Xendors approached with caution, looking for any signs of a trap. He didn't really think the gnomes were brave enough to try anything stupid, but now was not the time to test their intelligence.

Approaching the gnomes, Odin stared down at them, saying nothing.

"News we have," said the gnome sitting upfront.

"Well, get on with it," Odin demanded.

"The two you seek passed through Girk at last day light," he said.

"Are you certain?"

Their hair bobbed back and forth, as they both nodded their heads. Wicked grins spread across their scratched faces as they looked up at Odin, pleased with themselves. It was evident that the two had been riding through the shrubs by the injuries the branches had inflicted on them.

The two gnomes looked as if they could be brothers with the same beady eyes, and mouths that turned down at the corners. But, the only things they held in common were that they were gnomes abandoned at young ages by their villages, then rescued and adopted by Bondalin Jon Bardolyne, of Girk.

The gnome that spoke for the two of them was Brikdor Sed Gobamere. He was banished by the gnomes of Cheknorbin when it was discovered that the irises of his eyes were flaked with gold and red. This was a sign of evil, and the clan was fearful Brikdor would grow to be a deceitful tyrant, causing havoc amongst the village. As soon as Brikdor was weaned, he was placed in a basket, and pushed out to sea. For several weeks the basket bobbed along, until it finally made its way through an inlet into the rivers of Vesterra. It was then that Brikdor was rescued by the gnomes of Girk, and adopted into their clan.

The next season, after the great war, the gnomes of Girk found Fik Jon Henjor, wandering in the forest alone. After several attempts at finding his village proved fruitless, Bondalin decided to adopt him, also. It was soon learned that Fik was a mute. A gnome that could not speak was often considered an abomination, and useless. But, Bondalin felt differently. He believed there was good in everyone, and accepted Fik as one of their own.

Almost immediately, the two adopted gnomes bonded. Even though Fik could not speak, he and Brikdor communicated with gestures and eye contact that only the two of them understood.

Odin drew his sword and pointed it at the crooked nose of Brikdor. He was tired from all his travels, and his patience was wearing thin. "If I find your information to be false, I will slice off your ridiculous looking heads," he threatened.

Brikdor raised a finger and gingerly pushed the blade of the sword aside. "A lie we never tell," the gnome hissed defiantly.

Odin thought that they must be telling the truth because they were brave enough to stand up to him. "Very well. Here," he said, tossing them a gold coin. "More will follow once I have located the two."

They both looked at the coin, then looked up at Odin with furrowed brows.

He could tell they were not pleased that they were only rewarded with one coin. "Don't worry, I know where to find you. I always make good on my promises."

"See that you do," sneered Brikdor. Then he pulled on the hair of the boar, maneuvering it to turn. He kicked its side, and the boar dashed through the shrubs in the direction of Girk.

Chapter Twenty-five

The light of the morning cast a warm, golden glow through the branches of the trees. Aren stared at the leaves seeing visions of Inserpia's heads swaying in a deadly dance as the memories of the night clouded his mind. His sight came back into focus when Alexa stirred under his arm. After the attack, she had fallen into a sound sleep curled up against his sore body.

He watched as the lids of her eyes twitched, struggling to open. The corner of his mouth curled up when he saw her brows furrow and her nose scrunch when the stench of Inserpia's rotting corpse registered in her mind, jerking her awake.

"Eew." She sat up, covering her nose. Aren grabbed on to the back of her shirt, keeping her from falling off the branch.

"Stinks, huh?" Aren said, only half-joking.

She looked at him remembering what had happened. "Aren, are you okay?" At the sound of her voice, Bandit poked his head out of her pocket, then quickly retreated.

"I'm good. Just a little sore." He was exhausted, but his mind had refused to sleep. He wasn't sure how long he had sat there with Alexa asleep under his arm, breathing in the putrid smell of death. Time seemed to have stopped after Alexa had saved him.

"I can't believe I feel asleep with that smell." She crinkled her nose.

"Wanna get out of here?" he asked.

Looking down and around the tree, she tried to avoid eyeing the mass of gory carnage that was heaped on the ground below. "Come on. We can get down this way," she said, pointing at a lower branch on the other side of the tree.

Once they were on the ground, Aren put his hand on Alexa's shoulder, guiding her so she wouldn't have to look at Inserpia. They gave a wide berth to the rotting remains, walking around several trees before heading in the intended direction.

"Is that water I hear?" Alexa asked.

"Sounds like a stream somewhere nearby."

"It'd be nice to be able to wash up a bit if it is. I'd like to get some of this nasty blood off of me."

"I think the water is coming from over there," Aren said, jutting his chin towards a row of bushes.

His instincts were correct. On the other side of the bushes was a small stream that trickled between a bed of moss rocks. Alexa found a spot that poured like a faucet between two rocks and decided it was the perfect location for washing.

"Keep an eye out for me, will ya. I'm going to take my

shirt off and rinse it out," Alexa said, while coaxing Bandit out of her pocket, then removing her shirt. She looked down and inspected her bra. There was a small spot of redness that marred one cup, but she decided not to take it off to clean it, just in case. The water that soaked her shirt rinsed away pink as she rubbed it against the rocks. After she was confident that her shirt was free of as much of the blood that she could remove, she used it to wipe her face and arms, soiling the shirt once again. She rinsed out her hair, which was crusty with dried blood, dunking her head in the water. She cringed when a chunk of gooey grossness that was stuck to a strand of hair floated away. Watching the blood taint the water pink reminded her that she should clean her dagger also.

While Alexa was cleaning herself, Aren sat on a nearby rock inspecting the sword. The blue crystal was unblemished and solid. The blade didn't appear to have been damaged during the assault either, however, the scabbard bore a few deep scratches. He stood, lashing the sword in the air, wishing he had had the opportunity to use it on Inserpia. To make himself feel better about not having woken up before she had trapped him, he convinced himself that the sword was too fine of an instrument to be sullied with the blood of that beastly serpent.

"Did I get it all?" Alexa asked Aren, turning in a circle so he could see all the way around her. Her shirt was dripping wet, but felt good as it cooled her skin.

"Aside from your jeans, and a few light stains on your shirt, looks as if you got it all off," he said. "I think I'll rinse off also." He took his shirt off soaking it in the water, using it as Alexa did to wash himself. The cool water against his sore and bruised body was invigorating. He dunked his head in the stream, washing the blood out of his matted hair.

When he was finished cleaning up, he took out the wafers and offered one to Alexa, then sat next to her and enjoyed one also. As promised, the wafers made them feel full, and helped energize them.

Alexa was happy to see that Bandit had found a patch of flowers to munch on while cooling off in a little puddle of water.

Before starting out, Aren took out the book to look at the map again. He pointed to a spot and said, "I think we're about here. We've got two full days to make it to Rheyaros. Without any obstacles, I think we can do it."

"With Inserpia gone, hopefully, it won't be as dangerous." Alexa tugged at her ear.

"Hopefully. But, we do have the Xendors to look out for." He took one last look at the map, enlarging it. The image of the man at the edge of Rheyaros pointing to the north still puzzled him. He sighed and pocketed the book. "Let's get moving."

They walked for several miles through the brush and trees before Alexa decided to break the silence after noticing

Aren was deep in thought. "You okay?" she asked.

"Yeah, just thinking about things," he said.

"About what happened back there?"

Aren grimaced, his eyes downcast. "Actually, no."

"About Emma?"

"Is it that obvious?"

They were silent for a while. Then Alexa said, "Hey, I just thought of something!"

"What?" he asked, not really in the mood for conversation.

"Well, the dance isn't until the day after our birthday, which is tomorrow. If we're able to get the sword to our people tomorrow night, which is also the night of the Skylar Moon, then maybe you can get back in time to take her to the dance!"

Aren thought about this. "Do you think I could really make it back in time?" he asked, hopefully.

"Well, I don't know, but it's worth a try. Don't you think?"

"I think she is worth the try!" he said with conviction. His mood lightened as hope crept through him. "Hey Lex?"

"Hmm?"

"Isn't there, you know, anyone you like?" he asked, looking over his shoulder at her.

She shrugged her shoulders, biting on her bottom lip, suppressing a smile. The pink that blushed her cheeks gave away the fact that she was hiding something from him.

"So, there is someone!" he said, smiling at her. "Who is it? Huh?" he pressed.

They stopped abruptly in their tracks as several men, all dressed in green and brown, armed with sharp pointy spears, emerged from the bushes, surrounding them.

Aren reached out a protective hand, pulling Alexa behind him.

Alexa noticed her ears tingled, but didn't burn. *Weird.*

For a moment, everyone stood still. All were silent. Waiting ... until a familiar voice murmured, "Aren? Alexa?"

Alexa gasped. "Dain!" Excitement overwhelmed her as she pushed past Aren to step closer to Dain.

It was then that Aren learned exactly who it was that his sister secretly liked. The adoring girly look of infatuation that made her eyes twinkle, and, the silly smile that was plastered on her face at the sight of him, gave away her little secret.

Aren looked at his sister, then at Dain, then back at his sister again. *Really? Dain? Who knew?*

Aren was about to ask Dain what *he* was doing in Vesterra, but before the words even formed on his lips Alexa collapsed. Bandit squeaked in pain as he hit the ground with her, rolling off her shoulder.

"Oops," one of the men said.

"Alexa!" both Aren and Dain screamed at the same time, rushing to her aid.

“What happened?” Aren yelled at the man.

"I'm sorry. I'm sorry. I didn't mean for my spear to scratch her," he cried. "Her arm, it brushed against my spear when she moved forward."

Alexa was out cold, but still breathing.

"Is she going to die?” Aren screamed.

"No. I don't think so," said Dain. "It's just a nick. But we need to get her to the healer right away." He turned to the rest of the men and ordered, "Quickly, run. Advise Quelia what happened. Let her know we'll be bringing Alexa Rainz."

All but two of the men disappeared into the trees.

"Aren, can you carry her?" Dain asked.

He just nodded as he labored to pick up her limp body. He was sore and weakened from the crushing he received from Inserpia, but fear of losing his sister caused his adrenalin to pump, giving him the strength to carry her. She was like a rag doll in his arms. Bandit had managed to hop on top of Alexa's chest, where he stayed staring up at her face while Aren carried them. Aren wasn't sure if Bandit was injured, and he didn't have time to check. Right now, his main concern was Alexa.

"Quick. Follow me," Dain said.

Aren followed, with the two other men close behind. He noticed, but kept quiet, that the bushes and plants parted for Dain with just a wave of his hands. They folded back into place, unfazed, after the last man in the line passed. The plants seemed to be growing the deeper they journeyed, and soon the view of the sky was completely concealed. The sudden height of the plants gave the illusion that either the plants were getting taller, or the group was shrinking. Aren wasn't sure how Dain knew which way to go because there didn't appear to be a trail and the density of the area gave no clue of their location.

Although Alexa was relatively light, her dead weight was starting to put a strain on Aren. "How much farther?" he asked, trying not to sound out-of-breath.

"We're almost there," Dain said, giving Aren a sideways glance. "Are you okay? Do you need help?"

"No," he said. "I'm good. Just get us there." Stress was evident in his voice as he looked at his sister's non-responsive face.

Chapter Twenty-six

"How long?"

"Just several ticks. We were at one of the back trails when it happened," Dain advised Quelia. "This is her brother, Aren," he said, gesturing with his thumb.

Quelia stared into Aren's eyes for a mere second, then nodded. Her gaze brushed over the sword at his side, then she turned and pointed towards a downy bed. "Lay her here." Her voice was soft and gentle. At the end of the bed was a table lined with several small wooden bowls, containing different ointments and potions.

Aren gingerly laid Alexa down, then cupped Bandit in his hands, drawing him away. Bandit pushed his toes in between two of Aren's fingers, spreading them apart so he could see Alexa. Aren could feel Bandit trembling. "She'll be okay, little buddy," Aren whispered to Bandit, while petting the top of his head. *She better be okay*, he thought.

Dain gently gripped Aren's upper arm to guide him away from the bed. Aren shrugged him off roughly. "I'm not leaving. I'm not leaving her!" His voice was crisp.

"You don't have to leave, but you need to move out of Quelia's way so she can work. There is a seat right behind you," Dain said.

Aren cocked his head. A nest of twisted branches extended from the wall forming a platform for sitting. He backed up and sat heavily, surprised at how comfortable it was.

Dain took a seat next to him. "Don't worry. Quelia knows what she's doing. She is our noble healer. She's the best."

Aren gave Dain a sideways glance, then watched in silence as Quelia performed her magic on Alexa. Her lithe fingers pressed in a circle around the small wound, gently massaging the area. From one of the bowls, she sprinkled a pinch of fine, white granules over the scrape. As they melted in the wetness of the wound, they bubbled slightly before dissipating. Quelia then spread a fine layer of a nutty looking paste over the scratch with a flat wooden stick, then covered it with a small cloth.

After inspecting her work, she turned to Aren and said, "She will be fine. She will need rest. The wound is not severe. The effects of the toxin can cause disorientation and dizziness for several days. But, in time it will wear off completely, and she will be her normal self again." Quelia gave Aren a gentle smile. "She should wake soon. But, rest is her best medicine."

"Thank you," Aren said relieved, taking Quelia's outstretched hand. He knew that Quelia did everything she could to save his sister. He wasn't sure why, but something in him told him he could trust her.

While holding Aren's hands, Quelia turned them to look at the cuts on his fingers he had acquired from Dragon Fire. Without saying a word, she walked to her supplies, picked up a few items, then returned to Aren. She rubbed a salve on his cuts, then wrapped them in a light gauze. "These, too, will heal in a day or two," she said. Then she gathered the bowls, and quietly left the room.

Aren was staring at Dain. He had been wondering what Dain was doing in Vesterra but didn't want to ask in front of Quelia.

"What?" Dain asked, noticing the look on Aren's face.

Aren looked about and realized for the first time that the three of them were alone, now that Quelia was gone. Until now, he hadn’t even noticed that the men that had escorted them were no longer around. "Where did everyone go?" he asked, then said before Dain could answer, "I didn't even know they left."

The room they sat in was a large hallow in a tree. The walls were smooth, showing the tree's many layers of rings. It was so quiet, and peaceful.

"They are all probably back on patrol, after giving their report of the incident."

Aren peered at Dain as he thought about the swarm of questions that boggled his mind. In a hushed tone, so as not to disturb Alexa, he finally asked, "What are you doing here?"

"I guess I could ask you the same thing, but I think I can figure it out." Dain looked at Aren, then over to Alexa, and shook his head. "I didn't know you two were from Vesterra."

Aren quirked a brow. "I didn't know you were, either."

"Well, I guess by now you figured out I'm a faery," he said, looking around the room where they sat as if that explained everything. "Well, a half-breed faery, that is." He looked down at his feet.

"What do you mean by that?" Aren asked.

"My dad is a faery, and my mom is from the Other World. The world where we live and go to school."

Aren thought on it for a minute. "How did they meet?"

"Apparently, my mom was running from something, and fell. Somehow, she ended up here, in Vesterra. She hit her head and doesn't remember anything, not even what she was running from, or why. Anyway, my dad, who is a faery, and lives here, found her in the woods. They fell in love. I guess the rest is history."

"So, your mom lives in Mountain Springs, and your dad lives here?"

Dain nodded, and shrugged his shoulders. "It works, I guess." He looked down at his feet agin. "My dad visits us often, and I come here often, when I'm not in school."

Aren had wondered where Dain would go on his 'family visits'. Dain never really talked about it, and Aren never questioned him. "So, why doesn't your mom live here? Or, why doesn't your dad live there, in the Other World?"

He leaned back, slouching in his seat. "Well, my mom didn't really like it here that much. She liked the life of the Other World. After I was born, my dad agreed to let my mom raise me in the Other World to go to school, but, I had to come back here during school breaks to learn the ways of the faeries. They are still very much in love with each other, and see each other whenever they can. But, my mom doesn't come here anymore. Their relationship wasn't ..." he paused, "it wasn't very well received by the faery clan. If you know what I mean."

Aren nodded as if he understood. He looked at Alexa watching the slight rise and fall of her chest as she breathed softly. He wondered if she would still have her girly crush on Dain when she finds out he is half faery. Probably. After all, they were half-breeds, also. Aren didn't give much credence to one's genetic makeup, what mattered most was what kind of person an individual was. He was pretty sure Alexa felt the same way.

Dain straightened as a figure appeared in the doorway. They both turned to look at the man who Aren recognized as Dain's father.

"Dad," Dain acknowledged as he stood.

"Son." He nodded towards Dain. "Hello, Aren."

"Sir," Aren stood, walking towards him. He extended his hand, "It's nice to see you again, Mr. Ravend." He wasn't sure if they shook hands in faery-land, but it is what he would have done back home, in the Other World.

He accepted Aren's hand. "It's nice to see you as well. Sorry to hear about your sister." He looked at Alexa. "Quelia assured us she will be just fine in a few days," he said, with a half-smile. "I'm sure you two have a lot to discuss, but I need to speak with Dain. Please, son, come with me." It wasn't a request.

Dain walked towards the door as his father turned to leave. "I'll be back in a while." He looked at the doorway to see that his father was already gone, then turned back to Aren and whispered, "After he chews my ass!" He slapped both of his hands over the cheeks of his butt, as he jokingly grabbed them, appearing to push himself through the door.

Concerned, Aren raised his eyebrows in question. He wondered if Dain was in trouble, and if so, for what? He turned to look at Alexa and thought that maybe Dain shouldn't have brought them here, but there really was no choice.

Chapter Twenty-seven

"I understand you've had some visitors," Odin questioned Bondalin, while Drexter searched the entrance to Dragon Fire, and Glendon stood guard at the trail.

Bondalin said nothing. He stood as still as his shaking body would allow, while Odin pranced his stead in a circle around him.

"Which way did they go?" Odin demanded. Tension filled the air as Odin pulled his sword, pointing it at Bondalin. Still, Bondalin remained silent.

Out of the corner of his eye, Odin noticed Brikdor and Fik scurrying up a nearby tree. After meeting with the two gnomes in the morning, it had taken Odin and his men half the day to reach Girk. He was surprised to see Brikdor and Fik had also made it back in time to witness the inquest. But then, they were able to travel a more direct route, through the brush, on the boar.

The rest of the gnomes stood huddled in a group, under the cover of a large bush. Their fear for Bondalin mounted as they watched Odin interrogate the elderly gnome. They were too afraid to move, fearing any movement might trigger Odin into lashing out at Bondalin, or one of them.

"Speak! Or suffer the consequences!" Odin threatened. "Your choice," he said in a low growl, pushing the tip of his sword dangerously close to Bondalin's nose. Odin's agitation peaked at the lack of response, pushing his self-control over the edge. "Speak, I said!" His anger spilled as he raised his sword high. Descending his sword, the blade swung swift and true as it sliced effortlessly through Bondalin's hair.

The gnomes all gasped in horror as the twisted nest of hair detached from Bondalin's head, landing in a soft tuft on the ground at his feet.

Bondalin fell to his knees, devastated at the sight of his hair lying before him. The symbolic swirl of greying color that defined him as the eldest gnome, as the leader of Girk, had been taken from him. It now lay meaningless in the dirt. His sadness turned to hatred as he tore his eyes from the fibrous mound to glare up at Odin. He refused to let the tears go that threatened to spill. Until this moment, he had never truly felt hatred, he didn't think it was possible. But, at this very moment, he hated Odin with all his being. Involuntarily, his hands clenched into fists. He wanted to scream and tell Odin what he thought of his cowardly act, but knew it would mean his death.

Odin smirked, noticing Bondalin's knuckles as they turned white. "Dare to defy me again and the consequences will be worse." He turned towards his men. "They are around here somewhere. Search!" he ordered. He gave Brikdor and Fik a sideways glance, then sauntered off along the walking trail, leaving his sentries to their act of destruction.

Glendon and Drexter laughed as their horses pranced around, smashing all the trinkets that laid about the ground. They stomped through the bushes, trampling them down, causing the gnomes to scatter and run in fear. Drexter's horse reared up as a little gnome popped out of his hiding place in the bushes right in front of him. The small gnome tripped and fell just as the horse's powerful hoof dropped, landing on top of his leg. A bone crunching sound was heard, as the innocent victim screamed in pain.

Bondalin, reacting to the young victim's cries of anguish, grabbed a rock and threw it as hard as he could at Drexter's head. He ran towards the little gnome, noticing it was Tyke Jon Demikor, the smallest of their village. Bondalin screamed at Drexter, "Get away! Go! Murderous beast!"

Drexter rubbed at the welt forming on his head while spinning his horse around to see Bondalin racing towards him. He was determined to teach the old gnome a lesson. How dare he assault a Xendor! It wasn't his fault the stupid little runt ran out and fell under his horse! Drexter prodded his horse to charge.

Bondalin veered, trying to avoid being trampled. The horse was too fast, and Bondalin's body collided with its powerful leg, sending him soaring through the air. He rolled along the ground, ending in a mangled heap several feet away.

Drexter pulled on the reins, as he looked down at the unmoving gnome. His horse pranced in circles, as he yelled to the others, "Let this be a lesson to you!" Then he, and Glendon, kicked their horses into motion, and rode off in a gallop to catch up with Odin.

While a couple of gnomes tended to Tyke, Damure tended to Bondalin. "Alive, he still is!" Damure announced. There was a loud sigh of relief. Then, two gnomes carrying a wooden plank appeared. "Carefully, please." Damure instructed, even though he knew they would be.

With great caution, they lifted Bondalin onto the plank, then strapped him down with a braided rope to keep him from rolling off. Once he was secure, four gnomes each lifted a corner of the plank to their shoulder and carried Bondalin to their refuge.

As they walked past Tyke, who was being placed on another plank, the little gnome reached his tiny arms out, crying, "Bondalin! Bondalin!"

It broke Damure's heart to see Tyke so distraught, and in so much pain. He knew that Tyke was Bondalin's favorite, although Bondalin would never outwardly admit to having a favorite. "Okay he will be, Tyke." Damure kept his voice soft and even while patting Tyke's hand. He hoped he wasn't lying to Tyke. "To the mender he goes, as will you, too. Strong you must be, for Bondalin."

Tyke's eyes welled with tears. He wanted to be strong, but he wasn't sure he could do it.

Damure gently pushed Tyke's chin up with a finger, and looked into his eyes. "Break us, the Xendor's will not," he said in a tender, but serious tone.

Tyke stared at Damure with tear filled eyes. He wiped at them with the back of his hand. Then, he took a deep breath, and said, "Break us. Never!" trying to sound as brave as his shaky little voice would allow.

A smile of approval spread across Damure's face as the gnomes carried Tyke off to the mender. His gaze shifted, and noticed a void in the tree where a few moments ago Brikdor and Fik had been sitting.

Chapter Twenty-eight

Alexa opened her eyes. "Where am I?"

Aren leaped across the room, and was by her side in an instance. "Lex, are you okay? How do you feel?" Bandit jumped from Aren's shoulder onto Alexa's chest.

"Aren, is that you?" She was trying to focus on his face, but all she saw was a blurry blob of black and white.

"It's me." His voice was etched with concern. "And Bandit. Can you see us?"

Her hand went to her chest to pet Bandit. "You're just really blurry." She tried hard to focus. "What happened?" She sounded tired.

"You were pricked by the tip of one of the faeries' spears. Do you remember?"

She propped herself up on her elbows, then shook her head. The gesture caused her mind to spin, and she tried to stop it by pressing her hands against her skull. "I guess I shouldn't shake my head. That made me dizzy." Her voice was thick.

"Quelia, the faery healer, said you would be okay in a day or two. But you need to rest."

"The faery healer?" She sounded confused. "I'm thirsty. My mouth feels like cotton. Can I have some water?"

She started to sit up, then plopped back down. "Maybe I should just lay here." Bandit moved to her neck and nuzzled her. He started to purr, which caused the corner of Alexa's mouth to curl in a smile.

Dain entered the room, asking in a soft voice, "How is she?"

"She just woke up. She's thirsty, and would like some water. Can you get her some?"

"Of course. Be right back."

Within a few minutes, Quelia entered the room. Aren acknowledged her, then held his palm out for Bandit to jump on so that Quelia could examine Alexa without him in the way.

Dain returned, carrying a tray with food and a pitcher of water. He poured water into a wooden cup and offered it to Aren.

"Tell me what you see when you look at me," Quelia said to Alexa, as she inspected her eyes.

"I see, I see a figure. You're very blurry. I can tell you have long white hair."

"Please, sit up. Now tell me, what do you feel?" Quelia asked.

"When I sit up, I feel dizzy." Alexa squeezed her eyes shut, but her head kept spinning.

"Do you feel any pain?"

"No."

"Do you know where you are?"

"No. Well, I mean, I know I'm in Vesterra."

"Okay, that is good." Quelia gently pressed her hands on Alexa's head, turning it slowly from side to side, all the while watching her eyes.

Aren noticed that there was a sudden curiosity amongst the faeries. Several poked their heads in for a quick look, or would saunter by appearing to casually glance inside the room. He wondered if they had been doing this all along, or if he just noticed it.

"When you touch my head like that, it helps with the dizziness," Alexa said.

"Good." She massaged around Alexa's temples. "You should be feeling better soon. In a day or two, the effects of the toxin should wear off completely. You are a tiny one, which is why the effect on you has been so strong for such a small laceration." She inspected the wound. "This is healing well. Rest, while you can."

Before leaving, Quelia said to Dain and Aren, "Let me know if she needs anything. In the morning, she may still feel dizziness, but her eye sight should be better. The symptoms may come and go."

"Thank you," they both said.

Dain sat next to Alexa with the cup of water. "Water?" He guided her hands to the cup and helped her take a drink.

She drank slowly. When she was finished, she said,

"Thank you, Aren."

"It's Dain," he informed her.

"Dain?" She cocked her head and tried to focus on his face. "Dain from school?"

"Yes. Dain from school," he confirmed.

"What are you doing here? Where is Aren?" she asked, obviously confused.

"I'm right here, Alexa," Aren said, standing next to the bed. "With Bandit."

She turned her head, but all she could see was another blurry figure. But, she knew it was her brother, she could tell by his size, and his voice. "I'm kind of tired. I think I'm going to lay down again."

"Yes, you should sleep," said Dain. "We'll be right here if you need anything."

"Aren, too?"

"Yes, Aren, too," Dain said.

"Don't worry, sister. I'm not going anywhere without you." Aren hoped his words made her feel more secure.

"Okay, thank you." She closed her eyes and appeared to have fallen asleep right away.

Aren sat in the chair, feeling the stress from the day's events start to ebb. He felt tired, but wasn't sure he would be able to sleep.

"You two have become quite the spectacle around here."

Aren looked towards the entryway in time to see a faery quickly turn his head as he walked by. "I noticed. Are all the rooms, or whatever you call them here, open like this? Do any of them have doors?"

"Some do, but not all. We can close off the entryway if you want. That will tell everyone, including me, Quelia, my dad, etcetera, that they are not welcome to enter on their own free will."

Aren shook his head. "Nah. It's okay. We won't be here that long."

Dain pointed to the tray of food. "I brought you some food, if you're hungry. It may look strange, but it really is good stuff."

"Thanks." Aren eyed the tray of food, but didn't have the energy to move towards it.

"Here little critter, you want a piece?" Dain held a piece of red fruit out for Bandit.

"Bandit," Aren said.

"What?"

"His name is Bandit."

Dain chuckled. "Bandit. Ha. That's pretty cute considering their reputation."

"Well, what happened? Did you get into trouble?" Aren asked.

Dain shrugged his shoulders. "Not really. The elders are a little upset that I brought you here, but they understand why I did. It was the right thing to do. Considering the circumstances, they're a bit concerned about our people. They don't want any trouble here."

Aren nodded. "I can understand that. We have to get back to Rheyaros by tomorrow night, so we'll leave first thing in the morning. I hope Alexa will feel well enough." Aren rubbed the hilt of the sword. "I don't really know how far away we are from Rheyaros. Do you? Do you think we can make it?"

"That is one thing that was discussed. The elders thought it best for our people not to escort you any farther than where we found you. But there is no way you can make it to Rheyaros without help. Especially since you are not familiar with the terrain. They are sending a faery out to send word to your people."

Their conversation was interrupted by Dain's father. "I heard she woke."

"Yes. Her vision is blurry, but Quelia said she'll be fine," Dain said.

"That is good to hear. Aren, we want you to know we understand the importance of your presence in Vesterra. We will help as much as we can. We have no quarrel with your people, but this is not our fight, and we do not wish to bring it here."

Aren nodded. "I understand."

"Thank you. I know that you and your sister are

friends of Dain. I can appreciate that. But, at first light, I must insist that you two part ways until this matter is settled. He is my only son. I do not wish to put him in harm's way."

Aren glanced at Dain who was glaring at this father. "Yes, Sir. Of course. I, uh, I just want to say that I appreciate everything you have done for Alexa and me. It won't be forgotten. Thank you. We'll leave at first light."

"Thank you for your understanding. I'll leave you two to talk."

Dain leaned forward with his hands folded in front of him. He watched his father walk out, then looked down at his feet, deep in thought.

"You okay, Dain?" Aren asked.

"I swear, sometimes he treats me like a little kid. It can be so embarrassing."

"At least he cares. Some kids don't even have that much." Aren thought about Emma. He wondered if she was thinking about him as much as he was thinking about her. "Hey, do you know how everyone is at school? Do they know why we aren't there?"

Dain looked at Aren with sadness in his eyes. "We heard that Nana passed away. I'm sorry."

Aren looked up to the heavens that weren't there. All he saw was the inside of the tree. He hoped, where ever Nana was, that she was in a better place. His heart ached at the thought of her.

"The gang thinks you are away for Nana's funeral. Even I thought you were away for the funeral. It wasn't until I saw you two that I figured out you are the ones this whole drama is about. I had heard the stories, but didn't realize you two were the elves that were in hiding." He looked at Aren, his eyes were transfixed on the wall across the room. Clearly, he didn't want to talk. "Anyway, they're all hoping you will be back for the dance, but understand if you can't make it." Dain waited for Aren to speak. When Aren said nothing, he continued, "They all think I'm out for a family event. I was asked, rather, told, that I had to come back to help guard the area, until the passing of the Skylar Moon. All capable faeries trained in combat were to be on guard until deemed safe for our people. I'll be going back to Mountain Springs on Saturday morning, if all goes well tomorrow night."

Aren knew he carried a great responsibility on his shoulders, but he wasn't sure he quite understood the magnitude of it all. With uncertainty in his voice, Aren said, "*If* all goes well."

Chapter Twenty-nine

"What is that smell?" Drexter covered his nose with his hand. The odor was strong, and foul.

"Obviously, something dead and rotting," Odin said, recognizing the distinctive smell. "We need to find out where and what it is before we go further. It could be who we are searching for." A smile spread across Odin's face.

"I can barely see. It's so dark out here," Glendon complained.

"Well, then, I suggest you open your eyes and your senses, and find what is rotting. The sooner you two find it, the sooner we move on."

Glendon and Drexter looked at each other. Of course they had the dirty deed of finding whatever was dead, while Odin stood back and waited. Together they urged their horses on in search of the offending odor. The horses moved slowly, and were definitely spooked. It seemed as if they were purposely avoiding a specific area.

"Drex, I can't get my horse to go to the right." Glendon tugged on his horse's reins, trying to get him to turn. The horse backed up.

Drexter tried to guide his horse to the right, too. "Me either. Whatever it is, must be over there. Guess we'll have to go on foot."

They dismounted, pulling on the reins urging their horses to follow. They wouldn't budge.

"Stubborn beast!" Glendon gritted his teeth, while trying to pull his horse forward. "Well, as you can see, they aren't going to move!"

"How about you go on foot, and I'll stay here with the horses," offered Drexter.

"No way! How about you go in on foot, and I'll stay here with the horses!" Glendon argued.

"How about we flip a coin to see who goes in."

Glendon put his hands on his hips, "Fine! May the best man win!" He pulled a coin out from his pocket. Before flipping it in the air, he said, "Call it."

As the coin tumbled in the air, Drexter yelled, "Dragons!"

The coin landed on the ground, bounced once, then stilled. They both bent down to look at it. "I can't tell if its dragons or swords. It's too dark," Drexter said.

"I can't see it either. But then, your fat head is blocking what little light there is from the moon, so move over."

They both jumped, startled at the sound of Odin's voice, "What are you two idiots doing?"

"Uh, well, our horses wouldn't move and neither one of us wanted to walk over there," Drexter gestured with his thumb. "Since the smell is so bad, we decided to flip a coin to see who would go," he stammered.

Odin looked down at them. "Excellent. Who won?" he asked flatly.

"We can't see if the coin is dragons or swords. It's too dark," said Drexter.

"Even better!" Odin sounded happy. Then his voice changed dramatically, "Both of you idiots get your tails over there and find whatever it is! Now!"

They could feel Odin's glare at their backs as they started to walk.

"Good going. If you would have just gone by yourself, we would have never gotten chastised," Drexter hissed.

Glendon pushed him with his elbow. "It's not my fault! Why didn't you go check?"

"Just be quiet and search." Drexter covered his mouth with his hand. "Ugh, it's got to be close. It seriously stinks!"

"What's that?" Glendon pointed at a dark mound near a tree. They both stopped and stared, not believing what they were seeing. "Is that what I think it is?"

Drexter gagged. He walked around the mound. What little light the moon had to offer through the clouds reflected off the dead eyes of one of Inserpia's heads. He turned and walked briskly back to Odin, with Glendon close behind.

"We found it," Drexter announced.

"Well, what is it?" Odin demanded.

He coughed, then said, "Inserpia. She's been hacked up."

“Interesting,” Odin said, looking in the direction where Inserpia lay. “After all these years Inserpia has been alive, tormenting anything that moved near the water, now she is suddenly dead. Chopped to pieces. Away from the river.” He wondered what drew her this far from the water.

“I bet it was those kids, they must have used the sword to kill her!” said Drexter.

“Probably so,” Odin said. "We'll rest here until the morning light."

Glendon and Drexter both protested, "Here? The smell is too strong."

"Get over it. We need to be able to see if there are any tracks that lead away from Inserpia. The light will be here soon enough."

Chapter Thirty

The night for Aren had gone by slowly. After Dain left, Aren spent most of the time considering the importance of his task. There were still quite a few things he didn't understand. He hoped he would have the opportunity to speak with his parents before the appearance of the Skylar Moon. He knew he was supposed to return the sword to his people, but then what? Was he supposed to just hand the sword over to someone? Was he supposed to do something special with it? And, why him? All these thoughts, and more, were swarming through his head.

He had spent time studying the map and rereading what Nana had written. When nothing new jumped out at him, he removed the sword from its scabbard, looking at it with curiosity and considering its importance. The blade glowed brightly, lighting up the room. As he turned it to and fro in front of his face, he noticed for the first time that the swirls on the blade appeared to spell something. *Jericho.* Nana referenced Jericho in the notebook. Apparently, the sword was named after the Mer-King, which would make sense if it was a gift from the Mer-Folk. Maybe Jericho gave the elves the sword. If so, it had to be very old, since Jericho died a long time ago. The sword didn't look that old, though. As he turned it down to look at the crystal, the inside of the stone turned liquid again. Aren rubbed his thumb along its solid, clear curves, puzzled by its transformation. The churning waves within were mesmerizing. Slowly it solidified, and he put the sword back in its scabbard. Tilting his head against the wall, he closed his eyes, his mind drifting to thoughts of Emma.

Several hours later, he woke abruptly. "That's it! I think I figured it out!" he said out loud. He wasn't sure how long he had been asleep.

Alexa stirred. "Aren?"

"I'm here. Everything is okay." He tried not to sound too excited. If he truly did figure it out, he couldn't think of a reason why he wouldn't be able to make it back in time for the dance. "Sleep. I'll wake you when it's time," he said to Alexa. It was still very dark outside.

She turned on her side. "Okay," she said groggily. Then fell back asleep.

He was amazed that she could be out so quickly, but figured the toxins must be pretty potent. Rubbing the sleep from his eyes, he sat up and retrieved the book from the satchel. Opening it to the map of Rheyaros, he enlarged the area, focusing in on the image of the man. Suddenly, he understood that it wasn't just a man pointing to the north, it was a merman! And, the blue dot was the Skylar Moon! "I got it! I think," he said, talking to himself. He was excited and wanted to tell Alexa, but he knew she needed sleep. Daylight was finally starting to creep through the entryway.

He tried to relax, but couldn't. Pacing the room, he envisioned what Rheyaros must look like based on the images on the map. In order to get to the island where the massive tree was, they would have to cross over the river that surrounded it. The map didn't show any bridges, and he wondered if there were any, or if there were logs, like the ones they crossed over two days before. Rheyaros shouldn't be hard to find with the large statue of a merman in front of the tree. Once he returned the sword to the merman, he hoped his task was done. Then, he could go back to Mountain Springs. The place he called home for the last thirteen years. The place where his friends were. The place where Emma was.

Alexa turned on the bed. Aren walked over to her and put his hand on her shoulder. "Lex?"

"Hmm?" She didn't want to wake up.

"It's time to get up. We have to leave soon."

Alexa groaned.

He shook her shoulder. "Come on sleepy-head, wake up."

"I'm awake. I'm awake," she said, as she sat up with her eyes half open.

"How are you feeling? Can you see okay?"

She squinted her eyes and looked at him. Then she

reached over and took Bandit off his shoulder and rubbed him against her cheek. "I can see fine. Sort of. Things are just a little blurry. But not bad."

"Are you dizzy?"

"Not at the moment."

"Do you want something to eat?"

"Yes, please."

The tray of food that Dain had brought in still sat untouched. Everything looked and smelled fresh and eatable, so Aren rearranged the food on the tray, then presented it to Alexa. Holding it in front of her, he smiled and said, "Happy birthday, Sister."

A broad smile stretched across her face as she looked at the tray. Aren had moved the items around so they formed the number fifteen. Alexa grabbed Aren in a hug. "Happy Birthday my big, little brother." That was her joke with him; he was her big brother in size, but little brother in age, born just minutes after her.

He watched her take a bite of a fruit that looked like a purple raspberry.

She gave a little taste to Bandit who had been waiting expectantly. "Want some?" she asked Aren, pointing toward the food. Together in silence, they sat and ate until the plate was empty, sharing little bits with Bandit.

"We need to get going soon," Aren commented.

Alexa nodded her head in understanding. "Whoa."

"What's wrong?" Aren asked, concerned.

She squeezed her eyes closed. "I just got a little dizzy when I nodded."

There was a knock at the entrance. Both turned to see Dain entering the room. "Hey, guys. How's it going?"

"She's better," Aren said, looking towards Alexa. She had that silly grin plastered on her face again, and she was trying to untangle her hair with her fingers, as she looked at Dain. "She just had a little dizzy spell. And clearly her eyesight isn't one hundred percent yet." He teased, unsure if either of them caught his joke. *Really? Dain? The dude never even combs his hair, Alexa!*

Dain smiled at Alexa. "Hey, Lex. I'm glad to see you're up and doing better."

He just called her Lex!

She tilted her head to the side, and said with a bashful smile, "Thank you." She cocked her head and looked at Dain as a thought occurred to her.

"What?" Dain asked.

"Well, um, what are you doing here? In Vesterra, I mean."

Dain looked at Aren. Then Aren responded, "It's a long story, Sis. I'll explain it to you on our way. We really need to get going if we are going to make it all the way to Rheyaros before tonight." He reached his hand out to help her off the bed.

She stood, a little unsteady at first. "I'm fine." She took a step forward to prove it, and instead, moved involuntarily several steps to the side.

Aren reached out and grabbed hold of her arm, as Dain rushed in to help keep Alexa from falling over. "I got her," Aren said protectively. "Come on Alexa, I'll walk with you."

"Good idea," Alexa said.

Dain nodded with his head toward the entryway, "Follow me. Korbu would like to meet you two, and have a few words."

Aren asked, "Who is Korbu?"

"He's one of the elders," was all Dain said.

Walking outside the room, both Aren and Alexa looked about in awe. The place was a paradise. Huge willowy trees painted the sky. Their dangling branches were covered in delicate, pale green leaves that rustled melodiously like a natural wind chime. Beautiful plants grew along tiers of boulders that bordered numerous waterfalls. Small white birds soared from tree to tree turning gracefully as if performing an aerial ballet. Several faeries walked along paths that were hidden behind the boulders. A few had paused to glance curiously at the two visitors who were following Dain through the beautiful sanctuary.

Alexa wanted to take it all in and look around, but kept losing her balance whenever she looked up. She wanted to watch the birds perform their waltz.

Aren gripped her arm a little firmer to keep her steady. "Lex, maybe you can come back and see this place some other time." The thought of her coming back here and spending time with Dain bugged him for some unknown reason. Dain was their friend, so he wasn't sure why he would be bothered. Maybe it was the idea of him possibly becoming Alexa's boyfriend. He briefly wondered if he would be irked no matter who it was that Alexa liked. Speaking in a low voice, he reminded her, "Right now, we don't have time to sightsee."

She nodded as they followed Dain through a large archway of tangled vines. The entryway walls curved, giving the initial appearance that it would form a tunnel, but rounding the corner it opened up to a spacious courtyard. Flat slate rocks of various shapes and sizes decorated the ground. A low wall with vine covered columns outlined a section of the courtyard where three faeries stood waiting. Aren recognized Dain's father, and Quelia, and assumed the third to be Korbu.

"Aren, Alexa, you've met Quelia, and already know my father." Dain stretched his hand towards the third faery, "This is Korbu, one of our counsel elders."

Korbu stood erect, with his hands behind his back. He was tall and lean, like a stalk. His long, grey hair was pulled tightly back into a braid which seemed to cause his bushy, grey eyebrows to pull up in a point on his tall forehead. The irises of his slightly slanted eyes were so big and dark, hardly any white was visible around them. Under his long slender nose, thin lips turned down in a permanent frown. With barely any movement from his lips, he nodded slightly to the twins, and said, "Good early light to you two."

Aren was surprised at how soft and melodic Korbu's voice was. It didn't seem to match his stern features. "Good morning," Aren said. He gave Alexa a sideways glance and noticed she was standing very close to Dain, with that look of girly infatuation in her eyes.

"It is with dismay that we must have you part so quickly. I hope you understand that the circumstances at the present do not allow us to adequately accommodate guests hospitably," Korbu said.

Aren couldn't help staring at Korbu's lips as he talked. He thought it was amazing that his words were so well enunciated even though his lips hardly moved. "We understand," Aren said, speaking for the both of them.

"A company will escort you to an artery that will lead you to a passage which will take you in your intended direction. From there, we bid you a safe journey to Rheyaros." Korbu bowed slightly.

Aren shifted his stare from Korbu's lips, and tried to look directly at his eyes. "Thank you. We appreciate your help."

"Unfortunately, time is of the essence." Korbu lifted his hand, waving it slightly to point in the direction behind Aren and Alexa.

Aren turned his head to find a small group of faeries standing at the edge of the courtyard. He did not hear them approach. Clearly, Korbu wanted them to leave immediately. Aren figured the appearance of this group must be their cue to depart.

"Come on Alexa, it's time to go." He reached for Alexa's hand as she waved goodbye to Dain with that silly smile on her face. Since Dain made no effort to move, Aren figured he wasn't allowed to accompany the group. Aren nodded towards Dain, and said, "Later."

Dain just stood and stared, nodding his head in a silent agreement to see his friends later.

Chapter Thirty-one

Aren followed the group of faeries though the maze of plants with Alexa holding his hand, walking closely behind him. No one spoke, which gave Aren time to ponder what it was that was nagging at him. Something, he wasn't sure what, was off, but he couldn't quite place it. And then suddenly, it dawned on him; It was how quiet all the people and creatures in Vesterra could be. They never heard Krug sneak up behind them when he snatched the two in his arms and drug them into his cave. They didn't hear Inserpia until she had Aren completely wrapped. He didn't hear the faeries arrive at the courtyard. And now, the only noise that was being made was the sound of Aren and Alexa's footsteps, and the brush of the leaves as they moved. The faeries were nearly silent. They were walking so lightly on their feet, it seemed as if they were floating. He thought that maybe he was losing his hearing, but knew that couldn't be correct because everything else sounded normal. It was one more of those mystical things about Vesterra that he would have to get used to.

Aren nearly bumped into the guy in front of him as they all stopped without warning. He looked around to the faery in the front of the line watching him slowly part the plants, then step between them, disappearing behind the wall of greenery. All the other faeries stood quietly and waited. Aren was about to ask what was going on when the faery returned, motioning for the group to follow. They stepped out of the plants onto a narrow path. Still silent, Aren watched as they all lined up along the path, every other one facing the opposite direction. To Aren's surprise, Korbu appeared out of the plants behind Alexa, causing him to jump a bit. He never heard him coming and wondered if he had been behind them the whole time.

"Did I frighten you?" Korbu asked, peering at Aren with his strange eyes.

Aren admitted, "I didn't know you were behind us." Aren looked at Alexa who didn't seem to be disturbed by Korbu's sudden appearance. She seemed to not have a care in the world as she looked around at all the plants, and faeries.

Korbu looked at Alexa for a moment, then said to Aren, "You must be worried about her, but be assured, the toxin will wear off soon."

Aren glared at Korbu. "I hope so. I need to be able to get her to Rheyaros safely."

Korbu nodded in understanding. He reached behind his back and pulled forward a bow and quiver with arrows. "For you, a gift."

Aren was surprised, yet heartened by the gesture.

"Thank you," he said, reaching for the bow. The design seemed simple and a little antiquated compared to what he had been using in the Other World. But, he was sure he would not have a problem putting it to good use if need be. It felt like the right weight and size for him. He definitely felt more comfortable using a bow than a sword.

"And, one for Alexa," Korbu said, handing the smiling Alexa a smaller bow and quiver.

"Wow! Thank you," Alexa said, almost falling over reaching for it.

Aren grabbed on to her arm to steady her, wondering if she was stable enough to have such a weapon in her current state. But then, she did also have the dagger. He helped her position her quiver and bow around her back as the faeries had, and then did the same with his.

Korbu motioned to one of the four narrow pathways that branched out from where they stood. "This path will lead you toward the main trail to Rheyaros. Follow the main path, opposite the sun. We wish you well."

Aren thought he detected a smile from Korbu, but it was hard to tell. Taking hold of Alexa's hand, he said good-bye to Korbu, and then the faeries. After walking a few feet, Aren heard Bandit squeak, and turned around to see Alexa petting him as he sat on her shoulder. He looked passed Alexa and noticed the faeries were already gone. Not surprisingly, he didn't hear them leave.

Chapter Thirty-two

The faeries hadn't gone far before Korbu was stopped by one of their messengers.

"Korbu! Sir! The Xendors! Keet!" The faery was clearly upset.

Korbu put his hand on the messenger's shoulder. "Twex, calm yourself and tell me what it is."

Twex took a deep breath. "Sir, the Xendors arrived as we neared the spot where we had encountered the two elves yesterday." He took a deep breath. "They have Keet."

"Was the message delivered?" Korbu asked.

The faery shook his head, "No, sir."

Without another word, Korbu raised his arm for the other faeries to follow, then they dashed through the shrubs towards the area where Aren and Alexa were found the day before. Korbu had been afraid that something might happen to the two messengers. They were young, and inexperienced. But, they were the only two the elders were willing to spare. Though the task was no doubt dangerous, the faeries felt they needed to try and deliver a message to one of the elves, and point them in the right direction as to where Aren and Alexa would be. Unfortunately, with the failed attempt, Aren and Alexa were on their own.

Korbu suddenly appeared, standing on a large rock in front of Odin. He stood stern with his hands crossed in front of him, tucked away inside the sleeves of his robe. He said nothing, as he glared at Odin, eyes not blinking. The other faeries stayed back in the shrubs, out of sight, with their arrows trained on the Xendors.

Although Odin could sense the presence of the other faeries, he could not see them. He nudged his horse forward, stopping a few feet in front of Korbu. Then, he dropped Keet in a heap at the base of the rock. "I found him poaching in the woods," Odin lied. "He nearly killed a deer, but it managed to get away." Odin knew capturing a faery was the only way to get others to appear in the open.

Korbu remained silent. He knew the accusation was false. None of the faeries had ever killed a forest animal, not for food, nor for sport.

Odin decided not to waste any more time, and got to the point. "Have you had any visitors of recent?"

Korbu was unmoving, his eyes never faltering, not even to look down at the injured faery.

Odin realized Korbu was not going to come forth with any information. "No matter," he said. "We will find them soon enough. And when we do, expect us to meet again."

Korbu knew what Odin said was meant to be a threat, but he didn't react to his words. Instead, he stood motionless, never averting his eyes.

Odin turned his horse dangerously close to Keet, nearly trampling his head. As his horse turned, its tail brushed against Korbu, but he was unfazed.

It wasn't until the Xendors were out of sight before Korbu lowered to check the welfare of Keet.

At the feel of Korbu's touch, Keet looked up, his voice weak with despair, “I failed. I ... I am shameful."

"No mind," Korbu said. Then, he motioned for the others to come out. He felt sorry for the young faery knowing how inferior and inadequate he must be feeling.

Without being told, two of the faeries picked up Keet, who was unable to walk on his own. Apparently, Odin had allowed his men to beat the faery hoping to get some information out of him. But, the faery held silent, as was notorious of their kind.

Chapter Thirty-three

"Alexa, remember to tell me if you feel anything different with your ears," Aren reminded her.

"I will," she said. But, Aren wasn't sure if in her current state she would even recognize that her ears were burning.

By the time they had reached the main trail, it was already mid-day. Aren noticed the path to the left would have taken them directly into the sun.

Let's take a break for a minute. I want to look at the map to try and figure out where we are," Aren said, guiding Alexa to a large rock that was perfect for both of them to sit on.

They sat back-to-back. Alexa played with Bandit while Aren looked at the map. He had no idea where they were, but guessed they were east of Dragon Fire, and quite a bit south of Rheyaros. He was trying to focus on the narrow lines that depicted the trails, but Alexa kept squirming and jerking behind him.

"Alexa, keep still, I can't read the map with you gyrating around like that."

She was swatting her hands near her head. "I can't help it! These stupid bugs won't leave me alone!"

"What bugs?" Aren asked. There weren't any bugs bothering him.

"Ouch! They keep biting my ears!" Alexa cried.

Aren jumped up, spinning, looking at his sister's ears. They were flaming red! Nearly on fire! Aren moved in front of Alexa, reaching for his bow, but it was too late. Before he could pull an arrow, three Xendors appeared on their horses in front of them.

"Well, well, well. Look at who we have here," Odin smiled broadly at the twins.

Aren looked around for an escape route.

"We've been looking for you two for quite some time now." Odin was smiling like a Cheshire cat, as were his two sentries. Odin's eyes went from Aren's to the sword. The sight of it seemed to render him speechless as an odd look covered his face. Then suddenly, he bowed to Aren.

Drexter and Glendon, who were on either side of Odin, were confused by his behavior and wondered if they were supposed to bow, also. Then, out of the corner of his eyes, Glendon noticed something fluttering behind Odin. Realizing what it was, he yelled, "He's been stuck!" An arrow protruded from his back. He wasn't bowing to Aren, Glendon realized, he was dying!

Both Xendors pulled their swords, spinning around on their horses, looking for the culprit, but could see no one. Another arrow flew through the air whizzing past Glendon's head. The two sentries, hugged in close to Odin, trying to protect him. Glendon grabbed hold of the reins on Odin's horse, guiding it as the three charged from the area.

With the Xendors distracted, Aren had taken the opportunity to run. He grabbed hold of Alexa's hand and ran through the bushes afraid she might fall. His fears were realized when she slipped from his grasp and fell flat on her face. A stab of despair rocked through him wondering if she had also been shot with an arrow. Thankfully, she was okay, and was able to whisper to Aren that she had just lost her balance. He didn't know who was firing off arrows, and whether or not it was a friend or foe. If the sword was that important, more enemies, other than Odin, could be on the hunt for it. What he did know was that he needed to get his sister out of the line of fire, and to safety.

"Alexa, we need to hurry. Okay? We need to run," Aren whispered, with a sense of urgency. "Do you understand what is happening?"

Her eyes seemed unfocused, but she managed to say, "Yes, I understand."

"Okay. I really need you to concentrate. Concentrate on running, and following me."

She looked in her pocket to make sure Bandit was still alive and well, then she said, "Okay. I can do it. I think."

Aren took her hand and ran through the bushes as fast as he thought they could manage. He had no idea where he was going or if he was even running in the right direction, but he knew he was running away from the sun. After they had run for what Aren was sure was nearly a mile, they crossed over a trail, and stopped, both breathing hard.

He looked at Alexa's ears that were no longer red. He was slightly annoyed at her, and said, "Lex, those weren't bugs attacking you back there! It was your ears burning because the Xendors were near! I need you to focus and pay more attention. They could have killed us!" As soon as the words left his mouth, and he saw the distraught look on his sister's face, he regretted saying them. He felt like such a jerk. Of course she wouldn't know her ears were burning, the toxins are confusing her. "Sorry, Lex. I'm not mad at you. I'm mad at myself for letting my guard down, again."

"Are we almost home?" Her voice trembled.

Looking around, he said, "Honestly, I have no idea." Since he wasn't familiar with the area, he wasn't sure if they had run towards Rheyaros, or away from it. He led Alexa to a stump, and sat on a rock just above her. From there, he could keep her ears in his peripheral vision while also looking at the map. After a few frustrating moments of scanning the page, he slammed the book closed and let out a heavy sigh. If he had read the map correctly, he wasn't sure how they were going to make it to Rheyaros before tonight.

"*Psst*. Aren. Alexa."

Aren jumped at the mention of their names, nearly knocking Alexa over. Just then, Dain emerged from the bushes. "Hey, guys," Dain said, looking around guardedly.

"Dain! What are you doing here?" Aren asked.

Without answering, Dain looked around to Alexa, "Hey, Lex."

There he goes calling her Lex, again! And, there she goes waving to him all cutesy like, with that stupid smile on her face! "So, what are you doing here, Dain? Won't you get in trouble for being here? Aren't you supposed to be guarding your village?" The questions spewed from Aren's mouth.

"Yeah, but, one of the guys came back in a huff. The Xendors had injured one of our faeries trying to get information out of him about you two. From what he had said, I thought they were going to be heading in your direction. So, I couldn't just sit around and do nothing. I snuck out. Then, I sent a bird to try and find you. Did you notice it circling above?" Dain asked.

Aren looked up to the sky. "Um, no." Then he said, "The Xendors did find us! But someone shot the big dude in the back with an arrow! We took off running, since we didn't know who shot him. We were lucky to get away. It was a close call."

"Wow!" His eyes widened in surprise. "Well, I'm glad you escaped them and are safe. Anyway, I thought I would try to help. I can't go all the way to Rheyaros with you, but I brought a, uh, friend, that might be able to get you closer, faster." He raked his fingers through his tussled hair.

"A friend?" Aren questioned. "Does your friend fly, and can it carry us?"

"Well, he doesn't fly, but he can carry you," Dain smirked.

Aren saw movement behind Dain, and leaned to get a better look. He gasped. "Dain! Look out! Behind you!" Aren yelled. He reached for the sword.

Dain seemed unfazed. "Aren, it's okay." He turned, and waved his hand forward encouraging the creature to come out. A huge wolfish looking animal stepped out of the bushes. It was pure white with black stripes, like that of a snow-tiger, but its face and body were definitely that of a wolf, but bigger. "This is Zenith."

Zenith slinked out from behind the bushes, barely making a sound. He paced low, back and forth behind Dain a few times, never taking his icy blue eyes off Aren. Finally, he settled down next to Dain, sitting with regal eminence. Even sitting, the wolf was taller than Dain who had to reach up to scratch him behind the ears.

Aren's heart was beating out of his chest. Next to Inserpia, this had to be one of the most frightening creatures he had ever seen. Aren's faced registered shock when he heard his sister say, "Aw, a puppy. How cute. Can I pet it?"

Dain smiled, and reached his hand out for Alexa. "Sure."

"Be careful Alexa," warned Aren. He placed his hand

on the hilt of his sword.

"Relax Rainz. It's fine. He won't attack unless I give the order. He knows you're a friendly. If you weren't, he would already be picking his teeth with your bones." Dain guided Alexa to Zenith, placing her hand on top of his head where he knew Zenith liked to be stroked. Then, without warning, Zenith's massive tongue whipped out and licked Alexa across the face.

Alexa laughed, wiping at her cheek. "He's so sweet!"

Aren figured it must be safe since Alexa's ears weren't red. "Okay, Dain. How is Zenith going to help us?" Aren needed answers, time was running out.

"You two will ride on him. He's strong enough to carry both of you. The only issue is he'll stay in the bushes. He very rarely goes out into the open like this," he explained, waving his hands around. "He's quite shy," Dain smiled. "He'll walk really low, and close to the ground. You'll know when you get close to Rheyaros. He'll refuse to go any further." A serious look etched Dain's face as he stared into Zenith's eyes. "He gets very skittish around elves, and even faeries for that matter. During the war, a couple of these rare beauties were caught in the cross-fire and killed on accident. Zenith was orphaned. My uncle found him near his mother's dead body. Secretly, my uncle and dad helped raise him in the wild until he proved he was able to survive on his own. I was lucky. I got to help, and Zenith and I became very attached to each other." Dain smiled broadly as he scratched Zenith's head affectionately. "The grand-wolves were few before the war, but now they are nearly extinct. Which is the main reason they keep to themselves," Dain said, as he gave Zenith a final pat on the head. "Don't let our relationship fool you, grand-wolves can be very dangerous. Don't ever challenge one. Under the right circumstances, they can also be your best friend."

Aren nodded in understanding thinking how cool it would be to have a grand-wolf as a friend. He watched with a guarded eye as his sister made cooing sounds, and hugged the massive wolf. It was definitely beautiful, but also very intimidating. "Okay, so, how long will it take Zenith to get us to Rheyaros?"

"He should get you there around night fall. Don't panic if he stops suddenly, and turns around to go a different direction. He knows where he is supposed to go. If he stops, or turns quickly, he may just be trying to avoid startling someone, or something, or may be trying to avoid a dangerous situation. Grand-wolves are extremely smart, and very aware of their surroundings. To see one is a very rare sight. You should feel honored."

Although he thought this beast was majestic and beautiful, Aren had his reservations, but clearly, Alexa did not. Zenith seemed to be loving the attention Alexa was giving him.

"I guess you two should be going." Dain walked in front of Zenith and looked up into his eyes. "Zenith, it's time for you to take the A-twins home to Rheyaros. Take care of them, and of yourself. I'll see you later." Dain moved his hand in a downward motion which was a signal to Zenith to lower himself. Once Zenith was on the ground, Dain helped Alexa mount, then motioned for Aren to do the same behind her. "Lex, hold on to his fur around his neck. Aren, you'll need to hold onto Alexa. Stay low on his back, if possible. Good luck."

Before the twins could respond, Dain thrust his arm out and pointed his finger to the bushes in front of them. Zenith immediately scampered forward in a low crouch, walking as if he was stalking prey.

Aren righted Alexa when she slipped to the side as she turned slightly to wave goodbye to Dain, but he was already gone.

Chapter Thirty-four

The brush and trees whipped by in a blur as Zenith zigzagged his way through, avoiding open areas. Aren couldn't tell what direction they were traveling for they turned, and seemed to backtrack, so often. At one point, Aren was sure they had traveled in a giant circle, but it was hard to tell since the terrain looked all the same to him.

After sitting quietly for quite a distance, Aren broke the silence and said, "So, Lex, I think I figured it out."

Zenith stopped suddenly, and laid low to the ground.

The twins fell silent, listening intently. Aren looked towards Alexa's ears but saw no signs of redness. Zenith rose to a crouch, then started moving again, slowly at first.

Alexa asked, "Why did he stop?"

Zenith stopped again, with one paw raised in mid-step.

Aren whispered, "I have no idea. Let's listen and see if we can hear anything."

After a few seconds, Zenith started to move.

"I didn't hear anything, did you?" Aren asked.

Zenith froze.

Then it dawned on him, "Um, I think he doesn't want us to talk," Aren surmised. "It must be distracting for him, so

I guess we need to keep quiet."

Alexa gave Aren a thumbs-up, and nodded in agreement.

Once again, Zenith started to move in a smooth, stealth-like manner. Aren found it easy to stay fixed on the grand-wolf's back, but even so, he couldn't wait to get off so he could stretch his legs. Riding Zenith was similar to being on a horse, just effortless since no guidance was needed. According to Dain, Zenith knew exactly where he was going. How long it would take him to get there was the question that nagged at Aren's mind.

To pass the time, Aren decided to eat a wafer. He handed one to Alexa, also. She broke off a tiny piece, dropping it in her shirt pocket for Bandit. Popping the rest of the wafer in her mouth, Alexa moaned with pleasure, "Mmmm." Southern fried chicken and cornbread stuffing, another of the twins' favorites. The taste brought a pang of longing for Nana's home cooked meals, which were never to be again.

Aren noticed Zenith had slowed at the sound Alexa had made. Tapping her on the shoulder, he reminded her to stay quiet.

The day seemed long, and Aren wondered how much farther they had to go. They had been traveling for hours, it seemed, and the sunlight was starting to dissipate. Aren looked up and could already see the moon peeking over the horizon behind the trees. He nudged Alexa and pointed to the beautiful blue orb that hung low in the sky. She gasped at the sight. Just then, Zenith stopped, and sat on his haunches. The twins carefully slid off his back. They stood next to him, stretching out their legs.

When Zenith made no move to lower himself for the twins to remount, Aren said, "I guess this is it." He looked into Zenith's eyes for some sort of confirmation.

Zenith sat rigid, staring straight, not looking at Aren.

Alexa reached up and put her arms around Zenith's neck, giving him a gentle hug. "Thank you Zenith, and good bye. I will miss you. I wish you didn't have to go." As she let go of him, Zenith turned and licked her cheek. Then, he spun around and disappeared into the trees.

Aren looked toward the sky. It was nearly dark. They needed to get moving, but which way? He took out the book from his satchel to give the map one last look. Since Korbu had said "opposite the sun", Aren decided to keep the moon to his right, since the sun was no longer visible.

"Lex, we need to find the river. Once we find the river, we can follow it to Rheyaros. There should be a big statue of a merman at the base of a huge tree along the bank. Let's start this way," he said pointing, "and listen for the sound of water."

"Okay. But, what if we go the wrong way?" she asked.

"Let's not think about that, okay. Let's think positive.

If we don't find the merman, our people could be doomed. Now, keep quiet, listen for the flowing river, and tell me immediately if your ears start to tingle or burn." Before he started off, he reached over and gave Bandit, who was now sitting on Alexa's shoulder, a little scratch on the head.

Alexa grabbed onto Aren's hand as he led the way. They walked through a dense forest of tall spindly trees that had short branches and spade shaped leaves. Aren thought the trees were pretty, in an odd sort of way. Before long, he stopped. "Do you hear that?" he asked, in a loud whisper.

"I do," said Alexa. "It sounds like moving water. But, which way?"

"We must be going in the right direction since we can now hear the water, so let's keep going this way," Aren decided.

"Aren, my ears are starting to tingle!"

A look of concern covered Aren's face as he confirmed Alexa's ears were starting to turn red. So far, they were just slightly discolored, but a warning all the same.

"Lex, we're going to have to be very careful, and keep a good eye out for anyone. Can you do that? How are you feeling?" Aren asked.

She nodded, "I'm feeling better. I just feel dizzy every once in a while. My vision is better, too. It gets blurry off and on."

"Good. If your ears start to go lava hot, or even sun-baked warm, let me know by jerking on my arm. But for now, let's try to keep quiet, and only talk in hand gestures if at all possible."

She nodded her head in agreement. He reached for her hand and started toward the sound of the water. Soon, they came upon a row of bushes that blocked their route. Aren could tell by the sound that the flowing river was just beyond the bushes. Alexa tugged hard on Aren's arm. He crouched down, pulling Alexa with him. He turned to see her ears were very red, not as red as he has seen them before, but close enough that he knew danger was very nearby.

He motioned with his hand for her to stay put, then, pointed at himself, then his eyes, then the bushes. When she nodded in understanding, he crawled as quietly as he could through the brush. The only thing still visible was his feet when he finally stopped moving. After several very long seconds, Aren finally crawled his way back out.

Cupping his hands around her ear, he whispered, "I saw what I think is a Xendor that way on the river bank," his thumb jutted in the opposite direction that they intended to go. "We want to go that way. We need to keep low, and walk along the bushes."

Grabbing hold of her hand, they crouched and walked for several yards before Aren stopped to check the status of Alexa's ears. They were still the same shade of red which warned him there must be another Xendor nearby. Again, he motioned that he was going to crawl through the bushes to check. This time, Aren completely disappeared out of Alexa's sight. She started to get nervous when he didn't reappear right away. Unconsciously, she reached for her ears that were really starting to burn. Her heart started to pound. She didn't know what she should do. Should she call out for Aren, or quietly sit still and wait? Just then Aren popped his head out from the side of the bushes. He noticed right away the frightened look on Alexa's face and the brightness of her ears. He reached his hand to her pulling her into the bushes with him. They sat there quietly, listening for any sounds. Soon they heard what sounded like a lone horse walking slowly in the area. Aren wanted to take a peek, but was afraid of giving away their cover. Of course, it had to be a Xendor or Alexa's ears wouldn't have been so red. They sat for a few minutes until the sound of the horse's footsteps faded, and Alexa's ears receded.

Aren whispered into her ear again, "There's a gap, possibly an animal trail, between these bushes. Let's go that way. We may have to crawl to stay hidden. Try to stay quiet."

He started crawling on hands and knees, and Alexa followed. With every twig or branch they snapped, they would stop, and wait for a few seconds, listening for any predator's advance. By now, the sun had completely set, and they were navigating by moon light. The color of everything that surrounded them appeared grey due to the blueness of the moon. After nearly a hundred yards, the bushes stopped at the side of a large rock. The twins sat against the rock, rubbing at their scraped and bruised hands and knees.

Aren peered up at the moon, noticing a dark cloud that was inching its way towards it. That's when he noticed the sky was littered with small, gray clouds. Something told him this wasn't a good sign, but he wasn't quite sure why. Before one of the clouds covered the moon and took away their light, he checked their surroundings again by crawling through the bushes on one side, and then crawling through the bushes on the other side.

Sitting next to Alexa, he whispered, "I don't see anything in the trees over there, but the river drops over here, just beyond this boulder." He tapped it with his hand. "I can't see beyond that. All I can see is rocks. I need to peek over the top to see what's on the other side. Your ears are still a bit red, so we know there are bad guys around here somewhere."

Alexa nodded, not daring to speak.

Aren took a deep breath. While pulling himself up, a silly thought crossed his mind when his fingers gripped the top of the boulder; he wished his eyes were at the very top of his forehead, instead of below it, so he didn't have to expose so much of his head to see what was on the other side. As his eyes crested the rock, they grew wide, and he froze. Eyes that gleamed from the darkness of a cloak stared back at him.

Chapter Thirty-five

"Aren!" The man said in a loud whisper.

"Dad?"

Their dad vaulted over and slid down the side of the boulder between Aren and Alexa. He grabbed them both in a hug. "Shhhh. There are Xendors all around. Are you two okay? Thank the moon you are here!"

Alexa held tight to her father while Aren explained, "We're fine. Well, sort of. Alexa was pricked with a faery's spear. So, she's not quite herself."

He looked at Alexa with concern.

"It was an accident. Korbu said she would be fine in a few days."

"You met Korbu?" Erik asked.

Aren nodded.

Erik looked to the sky, then back at Aren. "I see you have the sword. That is good. You know what to do, then?"

"Yes. I think so," Aren said.

"Good. We're running out of time. Soon the sky will be one big cloud, covering the moon. The sword needs to be in its place before then. You understand that?" He kept talking. "I'm going to take Alexa to Yasmin. Your mother will be so relieved. When she saw Odin, and his two men ride up on you, she shot him."

Aren interrupted, "Mom was the one who shot that Xendor with the arrow?" He asked in shocked surprise.

"Yes, but unfortunately, he's probably still alive. Anyway, she tried to run to you, but you were too far away. By the time she reached the area, you were gone. Considering Alexa's state, I need to get her to a safe place. We'll head off this way. You can reach the island with the tree by crossing the river via the rocks, then follow the trail down. Be careful. The rocks can be very slippery. Once you are on the trail, you should be safe of Xendors. Don't get caught by one crossing the rocks. I haven't seen any this close, but they are sneaky." Feeling confident that his son knew what to do, he held onto Alexa, who was now hidden under his cloak. Without saying another word, he silently inched through the bushes and disappeared from Aren's sight.

Before Aren knew it, he was alone. “Okay, I can do this,” he said to himself. He crawled through the bushes along the side of the rock towards the river. Peeking through the leaves, at first he didn't see anything except trees across the river. But his gut told him there was more, so he kept watching. And then he saw it. Behind a tree, a Xendor was standing stalk still. At first, Aren thought it was the trunk of a tree, then he saw the man move slightly. He watched the man's head turn, looking in the direction where Aren was hiding. After a few minutes, the Xendor moved to the other side of the tree, looking in the other direction. That was when Aren decided it was time to move.

In a low crouch, he crept out of the bushes and tip-toed across the rocks as quickly as he could. The river flowed swiftly under the rocks, spraying a fine mist on top of them. He kept his eyes focused on the other side, gauging the distance at about forty feet. He hoped he could make it without slipping, before the Xendor turned to look his way. To Aren's dismay, a cloud moved in, covering the moon and blocking out its guiding light. The rocks in front of him became barely visible, but he knew he couldn't stop now. His toe caught and he stumbled forward. It took all his inner strength not to cry out in pain when his knee slammed down on a rock. He didn't have time to figure out if he was hurt, he needed to get moving, and fast. Only a few more feet to go.

Just as the moon was freeing itself from the cloud, Aren leapt from the last rock onto the trail. He quickly hid behind a tree, trying to slow his breathing. His knee was throbbing, but he had other things to worry about right now. He peered around the tree, and saw the Xendor was now looking in his direction again, but he made no indication that he had seen Aren.

Once the Xendor turned the other way Aren headed down the trail, trying to stay hidden by running from tree to tree. Half way down the path turned, opening up to a view that showed the island where the huge tree grew. Water flowed swiftly on both sides of the massive tree. The scenery was beautiful. This was it. This was his home. This was where his people lived. But, there was something wrong. Something didn't look quite right. The statue! Where was the statue of the merman? He didn't see it anywhere.

He crouched, looking about. The moon was shining bright now, lighting up the area. Looking closely, he could see movement here and there. Were they elves? Were they Xendors? He didn't know. Aren felt uneasy. He no longer was sure what he was supposed to do. He was expecting there to be a statue, a statue of Jericho, in front of the tree. He thought he was to return the sword to the statue. But, that obviously wasn't the answer. Deciding to take a moment to look at the book, there he saw it. The statue of Jericho was pointing to the moon. Aren's hand went to the sword. He looked at the hilt, noticing a tide churning inside the stone.

Aren looked up in time to see something moving along the rock wall on the other side of the giant tree. At first he thought it was two deer, but looking more closely, he determined it was two people. They blended so well with the backdrop he almost didn't see them. Then he noticed, it was his dad and Alexa. He could tell by their size and the way Alexa walked. He watched them disappear into the wall, then a few moments later, his dad came out by himself. He appeared to be looking around for someone, or something. A few seconds later, he went back to where Alexa had disappeared, then came back out without her and started walking along the wall in the same direction he had come.

Returning the book to the satchel, Aren glanced up at the sky. His heart sank when he saw the huge cloud cover rolling in, threatening to blanket the moon. He decided he had no other option than to get to the tree, and hopefully, along the way, he would figure out what he was supposed to do. Just then, a wiry man stepped in front of him.

"Aren Rainz?" The man was barely audible.

Aren was almost too afraid to talk. "How do you know my name?"

The man bent forward slightly, then said, "I'm Harbin, the elfin's Arch-Guard. Sorry, we don't have time for proper introductions. You must hurry and place the sword before the moon is covered. Follow me."

"But, I don't even know what I'm supposed to do!" Aren said.

"Quickly! Follow me. I will tell you."

Aren followed reluctantly. He wasn't sure if he should trust the guy, although, he really had no other option. He was going in the right direction, after all. And, he didn't look like a Xendor. Not that Aren knew what all the Xendors looked like, but the ones he had seen looked a lot meaner and dressed very differently.

Harbin was so quick and agile, Aren had to push hard

to keep up. They stayed off the trail, jumping over rocks, and going through bushes. Soon, they were at the water's edge. Harbin crouched down, Aren followed suit.

"In front of the tree, over there," Harbin pointed with a finger, "is where you need to place the sword."

"But how? Am I supposed to drive it into the ground, or what?" Aren asked.

"Exactly! You must do it while the moon is still visible. You must hurry. The clouds are threatening ..." Harbin's words were cut off at the sound of a wicked voice howling from across the river.

Mara stood tall on a flat rock, emitting an evil laugh. Her black dress flapped around her in the wind, giving it the look of bat wings fluttering about. In her right hand extended a wand spewing a lightning bolt that wrapped around a woman like a snake. Her prisoner was suspended in midair, trapped by Mara's powers. The woman's long hair touched the ground, but did not hide the spire she was being held over.

"Oh no!" Harbin said. "Not Yasmin!"

"Mom?" Aren exclaimed.

"Hurry, you must place the sword. The moon is almost covered. I will go to your mother's aid. You can cross the water by way of those roots." Harbin pointed at the gnarly roots that stretched across the water. "It's the only way to save your mother, and our people." Without another word, Harbin darted through the bushes leaving Aren to his own devices.

Aren gave little thought to the danger of crossing the river. He took off in a sprint, running across the tree roots as fast as he could. Before he knew it, he was on the other side, running towards the front of the tree. Nothing could stop him now.

"Mara! Release her!" Erik's voice echoed.

Mara laughed. "Give me the sword, and I will give you your wife."

"Never!" Erik bellowed.

"Then you will watch your precious elfin-wife die!" Mara threatened.

Aren was in a quandary. He couldn't bear the guilt if his mother died. But, if he didn't place the sword, all the elves would be in danger, and more of them, other than his mother, would die. Could he live with that? Looking about, he noticed there now were elves everywhere. Their bows trained on Mara, who appeared to be completely unfazed. Xendors were starting to come out of the trees.

"Aren, you must!" His dad yelled from across the river.

Aren's stomach turned. It was now or never. He raised the sword high above his head. The only sound Aren could hear was that of his heart pounding in his ears as the blade descended. With all his might, he plunged the sword into the ground.

Nothing happened.

Still holding onto the hilt, Aren looked at the sword, confused. Then back at the moon. Then at his father, and his mother who was still suspended over the spire that would soon end her life.

Mara's wicked laugh echoed. "It didn't work! He failed!"

All the elves looked on in disbelief.

Alexa had come out of hiding to witness the ordeal. She looked at the moon, then at Aren, then at the moon again. The clouds were rolling in, closer and closer, like a dark hand reaching to grab it. “Oh no,” she said to Bandit, “he's got it wrong.” She tried to yell to Aren, but he couldn't hear her. She knew she had to do something or many would die. Alexa nocked an arrow, and aimed. Bandit jumped from her shoulder into her pocket, shaking violently. Her vision was blurry, but she had to try. Standing as rigidly as possible, she released the arrow and watched it sail towards its target. With a loud thwack it hit its mark, punching into Aren. He slumped over, his hand sliding off the hilt of the sword, and down the blade.

Shocked silence filled the air.

Alexa looked at the sky. The moon was free of clouds.

The sword was now in direct line with the moon. The inside of the crystal started to churn violently, as it soaked up the light. Then, suddenly, a blinding flash burst from the stone, sending a turbulent wave blasting through the air. The force of the percussion blew everyone off balance as it discharged its protective magic. Trees swayed precariously shedding bark and leaves into the air creating a hurricane of debris.

Within seconds, the air settled, and then several things happened at once. Out of nowhere, Krug appeared wrapping his massive arms around Mara, causing her to drop her wand as she struggled to get free. The spell on Yasmin was broken. But before she could be impaled by the spire, Zenith bounded through the air, catching her in his massive jaws. He landed with grace belying one of his size, and carried her to Erik where he gently laid her down.

Erik scooped Yasmin in his arms, cradling her. "My love, are you alright?"

"Yes," she managed to say. Then, she remembered, "Aren and Alexa!"

Erik looked over to Aren who was sitting up being tended by several elves. Just then, Alexa appeared at their sides, along with Harbin, who was a little nervous at the sight of the grand-wolf.

"Mom!" Alexa screamed. Her mother held her hand out for Alexa. Alexa reached for her, but stumbled, and fell over. "I'm okay," she said quickly. "Just a little dizzy." Zenith nudged up next to her providing support, and Alexa hugged him, "Thank you again, Zenith." Then, she sat with her mother, and they held each other tight.

Alexa had told Erik about Zenith, so he wasn't worried when the he settled next to her. What did surprise him was the grand-wolf's presence. His children must have made a positive impression for Zenith to show himself. Hearing the struggle between Krug and Mara, Erik said, "Harbin, take care of Yasmin and Alexa. I need to help Krug."

Krug threw Mara to the ground. On all fours, she scampered toward her wand, and picked it up, waving it towards Krug in a threatening manner. Krug growled loudly.

"That won't work around here anymore, Mara!" Erik said.

Mara grunted in frustration as she stood. Her angry eyes darted around, looking for a way out. She started to run towards a Xendor who was approaching on a horse. The Xendor reached down, grabbed her arm and swung her behind him on to the horse.

"My powers may not work here, but beware if you, or your loved ones, ever wander from the protection of your little sword, my dear brother," Mara threatened.

All the elves cheered, waving their bows in the air, as Mara and the Xendors rode off into the darkness. Aren did it! He had saved their people!

Chapter Thirty-six

It had taken a lot of convincing, but Yasmin finally agreed to allow Aren to return to Mountain Springs for the school dance. But, only for one night! The last thing she wanted to do was to let her son leave after waiting thirteen years to have him home. She understood the commitment he had made to this girl, who apparently was someone very special to him.

The wound he suffered from being hit with the arrow by Alexa was not severe, however it did leave a nasty bruise. It turned out Korbu had stuffed soft, flat-tipped training arrows in Alexa's quiver, instead of warfare arrows. She had noticed them when she was in hiding by herself, and laughed knowing Korbu probably didn't trust her judgment given that she was still suffering from the effects of the poison.

The cut on Aren's hand from sliding down the sword when he was hit with the arrow required minimal bandaging. Luckily, his hand had stayed touching the sword when the light of the moon made contact with the crystal, or things would not have turned out so well. Little did he know, he had to be touching the sword for its power to work. Erik and Yasmin promised a grand story to tell about the history of the sword when Aren returned from Mountain Springs.

Under no circumstances would Alexa be allowed to go to the dance. She was still dizzy, and not quite herself. On the positive side, there was no question as to whether or not Alexa would be able to keep Bandit. Yasmin and Erik could see immediately the bond they shared, so Bandit was allowed to stay.

Aren should have been tired, but the excitement of saving his people from Mara's wrath, and being allowed to return to Mountain Springs kept his energy high. Harbin was assigned to escort him back to the Other World since it was unlikely that Mara would consider that the twins would return there. Yasmin and Erik figured Aren should be safe from the Xendors while in Mountain Springs, but wanted to send a guard just in case.

It was nearly seven in the evening when Aren arrived in Mountain Springs. He returned to the cabin hoping to salvage something decent to wear. Rummaging through his room, he found his slacks, but noticed a tear on the front between the pocket and the zipper. One of the sleeves on his shirt had a big shoe print on it that wouldn't brush off. No problem, he rolled his sleeves up a couple turns, hiding the dirt, then left it untucked in front, hanging down over the tear in his pants. He found a mirror in the bathroom that wasn't broken and checked his appearance. His shirt was slightly wrinkled, but hopefully, no one would notice. One thing he was sure everyone would spot was his shoes. They were caked with dirt from his adventures in Vesterra. He went back to his room and managed to find a matching pair of loafers. Finally, he was ready.

At the dance, Emma, Allison, Tara, Josh and Dain stood together talking in a corner. Tara noticed Emma kept looking at the clock that hung on the far wall, over the snack bar area.

"Hey, Emma, you've got two and a half more hours before your dad picks you up! Quit looking at the clock. Enjoy yourself!" Tara said, trying to get her to relax.

Emma fidgeted, wiping her hand on the skirt of her dress. "I am enjoying myself." She smiled. "I was just wondering, if maybe, um, the A-twins might be coming. I'd like to see them before I have to leave."

Dain wasn't sure if he should say anything. He finally decided to say a shortened version of what he knew. "I don't think Alexa will be here, because she apparently hasn't been feeling well. Which is understandable, considering Nana's passing. As far as Aren, he said he would try, but he wasn't sure he'd be able make it, either."

Allison asked, "When did you talk to them?"

"Oh, uh, I talked to them the other day, just briefly." Dain hoped they couldn't tell he wasn't being entirely truthful.

The DJ announced that he was going to liven things up a bit, and started playing a raucous upbeat song. All the kids in the hall went wild. It seemed as if every person was on the dance floor.

Tara grabbed the hands of two of her friends and said, "Hey everyone! Let's dance. Come on!"

The group followed, and soon they were all dancing in a circle around each other, with their arms raised in the air, having a great time. After a couple of songs, the DJ decided to slow things down a bit. Only those who were a couple seemed to stay on the dance floor.

Dain took hold of Emma's hand, and said, "Hey, Emma. Wanna dance?" He was gently guiding her towards the dance floor.

Emma was torn. "I, uh. No. I don't know how to slow dance." She wanted to dance with Aren, but he wasn't here.

"Come on. I'll teach you," he said, pulling her in close.

Emma looked towards the door, and around the hall, but still, no Aren.

"Relax. It's easy," Dain assured her. "Here, put your hands here." He placed her hands on his shoulders, then he put his hands on her hips. They swayed back and forth to the music. He could tell that she was starting to loosen up. "See, it's not hard, huh," he said, smiling at her.

She smiled back, "I guess." She really was having a good time.

"You're a pretty good dancer," Dain complimented.

Emma blushed, "Thank you."

"You look nice tonight, too." He looked admiringly at her.

Emma smiled, and looked down at their moving feet. She was flattered, but didn't know what to say. It wasn't every day she received a compliment.

As the song ended, Dain lifted her chin with his finger so she could look into his eyes.

When Aren arrived at the dance, everything seemed to be moving in slow motion. Standing across the room, he saw Josh, Tara and Allison at the same time that they saw him. For a split second, everyone seemed happy to see him. Then, their eyes turned to the dance floor, and their smiles faded. That was when Aren saw Emma. She was beautiful. But something wasn't right. Aren looked on, confused. Was he really seeing what he thought he was seeing? Or, were his eyes playing tricks on him? He tried to convince himself it wasn't real, but it was. Dain was kissing Emma!

ACKNOWLEDGEMENTS

A heartfelt *Thank You* goes out to all who have read this book. I hope you enjoyed the story as much as I enjoyed writing it. This has truly been a journey for me. If you did enjoy this story, please take moment to help me out by rating it.

A special *Thank You* to my editor, Julie Hauser, who put up with me over the past six years while I ventured into the realm of writing.

And I can't forget my family and friends: Melanie and Reece for your invaluable input; my husband, my mom, Chloe, Mary and Sharon, for all of their support; and my four-legged furry son (a golden retriever), Gixxer, who was by my side every step of the way.

www.ingramcontent.com/pod-product-compliance
Lightning Source LLC
Chambersburg PA
CBHW030620310726
48979CB00003B/803
9780999457924